TRAIL TOWN MARSHAL

Center Point
Large Print

Also by Todhunter Ballard and available from Center Point Large Print:

Tough in the Saddle
Badlands Buccaneer
High Desert

TRAIL TOWN MARSHAL

TODHUNTER BALLARD

Center Point Large Print
Thorndike, Maine

This Center Point Large Print edition
is published in the year 2023 by arrangement with
Golden West Inc.

First US edition: Popular Library

The text of this Large Print edition is unabridged.
In other aspects, this book may vary
from the original edition.
Printed in the United States of America
on permanent paper sourced using
environmentally responsible foresting methods.
Set in 16-point Times New Roman type.

ISBN 978-1-63808-936-0 (hardcover)
ISBN 978-1-63808-940-7 (paperback)

The Library of Congress has cataloged this record
under Library of Congress Control Number: 2023942202

Chapter One

Coming along the aisle of the lurching train, Joe Condon bent his head a little to avoid contact with the swinging overhead lamps. He was a tall man, and the high crown of his bell hat added inches to his height.

A woman with three small, hot, tired children raised a face made more unattractive by its layer of dust and soot. He nodded without quite intending to, drew a blank stare in return, and unconsciously quickened his stride until he came even with the seat which Lucy Warner occupied.

In contrast to the hot, exhausted mother, Lucy looked fresh and cool, and the gray eyes she turned up to meet his dark ones were level and calm, a trifle smiling, as if she shared a slight amusement with herself.

"Is your hoard still safe?"

He folded himself into the seat at her side, shifting the single gun he wore so that the heavy barrel rested on the stained cushion next to his leg. "All safe."

"Fifty thousand in gold is heavy."

He made no comment. He peered through the dirty train window beyond her. Outside, the flat-topped rolling sand hills of Kansas ran away southward as the train labored by.

She said, "Did it occur to you when you

brought it from the bank that you might have taken another train, say for the East, and lost yourself with fifty thousand dollars?"

He gave her a small grin. "That much money would scare me. I never expect to have five, let alone fifty thousand. Some men like your father are born to make money, others to spend it. I guess I'm the spending kind."

"On cards and women."

He did not deny this and she regarded his face with candid interest. "You know what they say about you, Joe?"

She saw his mouth tighten at her question, but still he offered no denial. Instead he said, almost harshly, "You have too much curiosity, Lucy. Stay on your own side of town."

"Does that mean you don't belong on my side?" She knew she should not be questioning him, but a girlhood impishness which she had never quite outgrown kept her at it.

"I'm on neither side," he said seriously. "Cap and I stand in the middle, as you well know. To be a peace officer in this country you can't afford friends."

She was still studying him. She knew his story well—for that matter, so did everyone else in Dexter Springs. He had come up the long western trail with one of the first herds to cover its wearing miles, and like a thousand other cowboys he had had his fling on Railroad Avenue, viewing the elephant from all sides in the gaudy saloons and dancehalls which girded its southern edge, and winding up a wild five days in the town's solid jail.

He emerged to find his crew gone, already having hit the dry, dusty miles which would lead them back to Texas, but he had not followed. His reasons had never been clear. Instead he had taken Cap Lennox's offer.

Cap was a small man, already gray in his early forties. He had helped build the railroad west, controlling its boom towns one after another as they mushroomed into brief glory, only to fade as the end of rail moved westward.

Why he had elected to stay in Dexter Springs, rather than move on westward through southern Colorado and into New Mexico as the grade thrust forward, was a mystery that not even Cap could explain. But he had stayed, and he had run the town with an iron grip during the two years he held the marshal's office, and one day, standing in front of the Western Belle, Dexter's biggest saloon, he had persuaded Condon to become his deputy.

"You're young," he said, "and there's a wild streak in you. Someone has hurt you badly, and you're fighting the world in return."

Joe Condon had gaped at the marshal, surprised that the man seemed able to read his mind.

"You need responsibility, the responsibility

of helping keep order in this town," Cap said.

Joe Condon laughed. "Me a marshal?" he said. "You're losing your mind, Cap. Come the first pay day, I'd get loaded and cause you more trouble than any man on the street."

"I'll chance it," Cap said. "I've watched you these last few days. You've a good head when you use it for something besides a place to perch your hat. You know how to handle a gun, and you're a good man in a fight." He rubbed his left cheek reflectively where the bruise left by Condon's fist had not yet faded.

"But there is more to it than that. You're a Texan and you fought for the South. Half the trouble in these trail towns happens because most of the people here—and the peace officers too—were on the Northern side. When the Texas trail crews hit town they try and start the war all over again."

Condon grinned. There was much truth in what Cap said. "I still don't think I'm the man for the job."

"I do. Try it for a month."

The month had stretched into seven. Joe Condon had become a fixture, a reassuring force to those nervous citizens who lived north of Railroad Avenue and who, as another season rolled around, saw the first herds arrive with increasing nervousness.

And yet to Lucy Warner, this Joe Condon

was still a mystery. She met him on the streets. She even met him in her own home where he accompanied Cap from time to time to confer with her father; but she realized that she knew him not at all, and this chance train ride offered her the first real chance to talk with him.

"Tell me about yourself," she said, "and the country you come from, and why you chose not to go back!"

A tiny up-turn tugged at the corner of his straight mouth.

"Don't pry," he said. "You already have your man, and a woman should never know too much about more than one man."

Her return smile showed that she was not offended, but it died as a voice from behind them said, "Joe was always good at telling a woman what she should do."

Lucy looked around quickly. A redheaded girl had come along the aisle and stopped behind them. Joe Condon did not turn, but Lucy noticed that his dark eyes had grown darker and his bronzed face had gone vacant, unreadable, like an Indian's.

This isn't the same man, Lucy thought, and gave her attention to the girl's face. She saw beauty there, marred at the moment by something which might be mockery, or anger. The green eyes glinted, although the lips curved in a slight smile.

"Surely you haven't forgotten?" the girl said.

Joe Condon stood up. "Where'd you come from?"

"I've been on this train since Kansas City, waiting for you to notice me. You've walked past my seat five times, and never so much as glanced in my direction."

He said, as if suddenly remembering his manners, "This is Kern Alder, Lucy. I used to work for her father."

"And take me to dances," Kern said. She sat down unasked opposite Lucy, and studied her with open candor. "I must say the Joe hasn't lost his eye for women. No wonder he didn't see me in the next car back."

Condon sat down slowly, all his ease of manner gone. "I never expected to see you in Kansas," he said shortly.

Kern laughed. It was a slight, rolling, musical sound. She's very sure of herself, Lucy thought, and very spoiled. She doesn't like finding me here with Joe. She doesn't like it at all.

"I've been in New Orleans," Kern Alder said, "and then New York. I'm to meet Dad in Dexter. He's coming up with one of the herds."

Joe Condon was surprised. To his way of thinking Pat Alder owned half the cows in Texas. He would not have expected the rancher to bother accompanying one of his trail herds.

"Dad's taking up some leases in the Nations,"

Kern said carelessly, "soon as he sells the herds he's bringing up now."

Condon said, "Is Rick Hampton coming too?"

She giggled, delighted. "Still jealous of Rick? Is that the reason you didn't come back last fall—or is she the reason?" She looked directly at Lucy who flushed in spite of herself.

"Stop your tricks, Kern," Condon said irritably. "Miss Lucy's engaged to Hartford Hull. I had to go east to fetch some money for her father and she just happened to be on the train. As for my not coming back, I told you before I left I wasn't coming back. I told you I don't play second fiddle to anyone."

He shifted his position and his coat fell open, exposing the star pinned to his shirt pocket. Kern stared at it. Then she burst into unrestrained laughter.

"Now I've seen everything! Wild Joe Condon a marshal! Wait until the boys with the herds get here—wait until they see it for themselves!"

The coach door opened. Jarmon Clark the conductor appeared. "Dexter," he called. "Dexter Springs next stop."

Throughout the car, people cramped from their long ride stirred and stood up. Kern said, "I'd better see to my things," and rose. She waited for half a minute as if expecting Joe Condon to offer to help her. When he did not, she gave Lucy Warner a too-bright smile.

"I'll see you later. I'll be in Dexter for several weeks."

She was gone, threading her way back along the now filling aisle. Condon did not look after her. Gravely he handed down Lucy's coat. He removed her carpetbag and his own small case and stooped to peer through the window.

The town came into sight: first the loading pens, already well filled with bawling cattle from the first herds to come in, then the scattered shacks, and finally the ordered rows of business buildings.

Still only two years old, Dexter Springs was growing fast and already its unpainted buildings were taking on a weathered look. The train slowed as it ran along the center of Railroad Avenue, and Condon had his glimpse of the saloons and dancehalls which lined the south side of the wide dusty street. They pulled to a puffing halt beside the station platform and he stood aside to allow Lucy to pass him.

She hesitated for an instant. Then she said, "Was she the reason you left Texas?"

He did not pretend to misunderstand. He nodded shortly.

"She's attractive," Lucy said, and knew she sounded catty and didn't care. She went out onto the platform and he followed, carrying the bags.

There was a fair crowd at the station, at least

a hundred people. Dexter Springs drew its life from the road and it had not outgrown the habit of making the station a meeting place at train time.

Lucy's father gave her a hand as she came off the bottom step. Hartford Hull came forward, his narrow, handsome face lighting at sight of her.

Condon knew a sudden restlessness and deliberately looked away from the girl who was not his. He searched the crowd for Cap Lennox—Cap being an inveterate train meeter—and was surprised when he couldn't locate the little marshal. He stepped down, handing Warner, his daughter's bag.

"Everything all right?" Warner asked.

"Fine," Joe Condon said, and wondered if he could ever be as casual about fifty thousand dollars in gold as the cattle buyer seemed to be. "It's in a box in the baggage car. Have you got a wagon?"

Lloyd Warner nodded and turned his head. "Bill, Bill Gilmore!"

The livery man pushed through the crowd.

"Give Joe a hand with the box," Warner said. "Here let me take that." He reached out and took Joe's case, and Joe followed Gilmore down the platform to where the baggage car stood behind the puffing engine. The baggage man slid back the car door.

"I'm glad to see that go," he said in relief.

Joe vaulted into the car. He signed the receipt, helped push the heavy box to the door, then jumped down. Between them he and Gilmore hefted it across the platform and into the back of the buckboard.

Condon climbed up beside the driver and turned to survey the crowd. He saw Kern Alder making her way toward the hotel hack.

Then he saw the woman and three children he had noticed on the train push through the crowd, followed by Sam Seller.

Condon frowned. He had heard that Seller had a wife and that she was expected to join him, but the children came as a distinct surprise. Seller was not cut out to be a father. He knew a great deal about the man. In fact, he knew a lot about the citizens of Dexter. It was part of the training Cap had given him.

"A marshal is something like a doctor," Cap had said. "If he knows the people and their weaknesses he can sometimes check them before they go too far."

Seller was one of the men Cap had watched. He was too good-looking, and he wasn't equipped to stand pressure. Sometime, somewhere, Sam Seller would come up against something too big for him and he would go bad. That's what Cap had said.

Seeing Seller reminded him of Cap's absence and he turned to Gilmore. "Seen Cap?"

Gilmore looked at him, then quickly away as he started the team. "You mean you haven't heard? He's dead."

For an instant Condon experienced no feeling of shock, and then the meaning of Gilmore's words rushed over him. He heard himself say, "What happened?" and knew even as he asked that he did not really care. Cap was dead. What real difference did it make to learn how he had died? Nothing anyone could do would bring him back.

"Somebody shot him," Gilmore said. "Nobody knows who."

Chapter Two

The marshal's office was in the southwest wing of the city hall a block above Railroad Avenue, across Denver Street from the new bank.

Joe Condon left the bank after turning over the gold box and crossed the street to the office. Blankton and Phil Moore were there, Blankton sitting at the desk, Moore lounging against the door which opened on the jail.

As he came in their talk ceased abruptly and he knew they had been discussing him. Blankton was tall, almost as tall as Condon, but his bulky body made him seem shorter. His hair was light, his eyes blue, a cold blue which gave them flatness. He was thirty, and he had been in town six months longer than Condon, and he had resented it when Cap Lennox chose Condon as first deputy.

Phil Moore was a kid, maybe twenty-one, with a slack mouth and narrow face. Cap told Condon that the boy was the son of an old friend, and explained no further. Cap had been like that at times. Close-mouthed.

"So you came back after all," Blankton said, and Phil Moore smirked.

"Blankton was betting you'd go south with the gold," Moore said.

"Too heavy to carry." Condon took off his hat and hung it on a peg.

"I suppose you heard about Cap?" Phil Moore said.

"That he's dead, no more."

Blankton had a small knife. He used it to pare the nail of the index finger of his left hand. "Is there more?"

Condon sensed the antagonism in the room. He was the first deputy. He was in charge now. He would be in charge until the town council got around to appointing Cap's successor.

They had been discussing this when he came in, and he did not have to read their minds to know how they felt about it. With him out of the way Blankton would stand a better than even chance of getting Cap's job, and Phil Moore would be his first deputy.

He wondered how long Blankton would last. There was a cold streak of brutality in the man which approached sadism. Given the chance Blankton would develop into a killer, and a killer could not hold a town. It took more than that, far more, to rule a town. It took understanding and a knowledge of people and their weaknesses. Cap Lennox had taught him that. Cap had showed him, even as he tried to show Blankton and Phil Moore. But Blankton had failed to understand because he lacked the ability to comprehend people, to project himself into their places and see their problems. And Phil Moore failed from sheer moral weakness.

No, there would be trouble when he left, and he had already made up his mind to leave. The idea had started on the train. Kern Alder's sudden appearance had thrown him. He admitted it. The girl had always disconcerted him. He had stayed north to avoid her, to escape from her.

But actually it was Lucy Warner who had made up his mind. He did not know where he would go. As yet he had formulated no plan. But as he had stood in the bank window he had seen her ride past in Hartford Hull's red-wheeled buggy, and immediately the town had become too small for him.

Cap was dead. There was nothing to hold him in the Springs. He hesitated, weighing the next move. His impulse was to keep the decision to himself, to let Blankton and Phil Moore wonder. He enjoyed baiting them, making them worry, but there were reasons why it would be wiser to turn in his badge now, to let Blankton take over, to free himself for his preparation for departure.

He said then, "I wonder who will get Cap's job?" and saw Blankton's eyes cloud as if to mask his emotions.

"I suppose you will," Blankton said. "You stand in line, and with Warner and the rest you're the fair-haired boy."

"I don't want it," he said.

He saw disbelief in both faces, and because he had studied them during the last few months he knew what each was thinking. Blankton put it down to pretense, a front for pride, so that if the position were not offered, no face would be lost. Moore put it down to deviousness, since Moore was a natural schemer, a man who played each situation with the hope of personal gain.

He smiled, a little mockingly, but he made no effort to press the point. Warner had spoken to him in the bank. Warner had said that there would be a meeting at his house within the hour, and suggested that he be there.

Actually it was an order, for Lloyd Warner more nearly ran the town than any other single man. But Warner was a believer in form, and it would not be his way to offer the appointment unless the full membership of the town council had duly approved it.

The house which Warner occupied with his daughter stood in a square of nearly grassless yard which during the summer months baked to a hardness resembling flint.

A boardwalk led from the street to the steps of the wide porch. Condon came up onto the porch, lit faintly by the yellow lamplight within, and saw the men in the big room clearly through the unshaded window.

There was the mayor, short and slight, looking somehow absurd as always with his goat-like whiskers, and Warner standing at his elbow, and in the background the three other council members. He had this moment to appraise them while he was still unobserved.

He knew each of them individually, but this was his first experience in being summoned to face them at one of their meetings. Cap had handled that. Cap had been rather jealous of his command and had frowned on any of his deputies taking orders except from him.

Joe Condon drew a long, slow, steadying breath and knocked. From where he stood before the door he could see Warner leave his place beside the mayor and move into the hall. A minute later Warner opened the door and smiled at him.

"Come in, Joe. We've been waiting for you."

Despite the smile there was a touch of reproof in the voice. Lloyd Warner did not like to be kept waiting, especially by those he considered employees.

Joe Condon had noted this trait in the cattle buyer before and had found it slightly annoying. Now it merely amused him, for he no longer considered himself an employee of Lloyd Warner, or of the town, and he took a certain small-boy pleasure in the fact that a few minutes hence he would be free to tell them all exactly what he thought.

He followed Warner through the hall to the entrance of the big front room. This was the largest house in Dexter Springs. Warner had furnished it as carefully as he could, but it still lacked many of the comforts to be found farther east. It was a silent reminder that this was the frontier, that in spite of the railroad which carried the cattle to market it was still remote, separated from the settled East by a good five hundred miles of sparsely inhabited country.

The mayor's name was Boyce. A small man who ran the hardware store and sang in the church choir on Sundays, he had a surprisingly large bass voice. But aside from his voice, the mayor was not notable for many things. At home he took orders from an over-sized wife, and in the affairs of the town he took his orders from Lloyd Warner.

He spoke as Joe Condon came in, but Condon merely nodded to him, as he did to Crafts who owned the town's best hotel, and Marvin Hale who ran the livery. These two were quiet men, content to sit silently by and let Warner make their decisions for them.

Hartford Hull was the one to whom Condon gave his full attention. Hull was seven or eight years older than Joe. He had been a major in the Union army, coming up from the ranks, and he had arrived in Kansas with one idea in mind: to establish himself firmly in the growing state.

He had helped lay out the town plot, and his newspaper consistently boosted Dexter Springs.

He came forward now, a smiling man, handsome in a slightly heavy way, to grasp Joe Condon's hand.

As their palms met Condon tried to decide exactly why he disliked the newspaper owner. Because Hull was marrying Lucy Warner? Certainly the girl stood between them, although as far as Condon knew Hull had not even sensed his interest in Warner's daughter. For that matter, no one had. He had been careful that none should find out, not even Lucy herself.

Hull used his free hand to slap Condon's shoulder. "I should let the mayor tell you, but I said, 'Gentlemen, he's my friend, as close a friend as a man can have, and I demand the privilege of telling him.' "

"Telling me what?" Condon kept his face immobile.

"That you're the new marshal."

Joe Condon could not have been less surprised. He had expected this ever since hearing of Cap Lennox's death. They think they're being generous, he mused. They think I should be grateful. There's not a man in this room who won't expect favors in return. To them a marshal is little better than an errand boy who keeps the peace and protects their homes and goods. Well, in this case someone else can have the job.

He started to say this aloud, but he never had the chance. Lloyd Warner had given Hartford

Hull his moment in the center of the stage, and now he resumed command.

"I hope you'll understand what I have to say." He had a presence, this father of Lucy Warner, and his voice had a reassuring resonance. He smiled at Condon as if by so doing he would take the sting out of his next words. "But at first I was opposed to offering you the position. Frankly I have nothing against you, but you are young, and your entrance into this town was not such as to invite trust."

Joe Condon waited, curious now to hear what Warner had to say.

"Oh, I don't mean that I didn't trust you personally," the stock buyer went on. "I would hardly have sent you to Kansas City to bring back that fifty thousand dollars if I didn't. But you were wild when you came here, and some of your associations since your arrival are not among what I would consider our better element. But none of that counted nearly as much as the fact that you were very close to Cap Lennox."

Condon was startled. He considered his association with Lennox the best recommendation he could have.

"I don't quite understand," he said.

Warner did something entirely foreign to his nature. He took two steps forward and placed a hand on Condon's shoulder.

"I hate to tell you this, for it is apparent that

you haven't heard. I respected Cap as much as any man in town, but there has been nothing but trouble ever since you left."

Condon's lips were suddenly too dry and the muscles of his throat seemed to be contracting. "What are you trying to say?"

"Another herd came in two days after you left. They were jumped twenty miles south of town, and the trail boss claimed that they lost five hundred head. They came riding into town, eight of them, with blood in their eyes. Cap threw four of them into jail and ran the rest out."

"That was his job," Condon said tonelessly. "To keep the peace."

"I know it, Joe, but we can't have trouble with the trail herds. This town lives for one thing and one thing only—to ship beef."

"I don't understand what you are accusing Cap of," Joe Condon said. "You want your wives protected, and your daughters and your property. You set up Railroad Avenue as a deadline which the trail riders are not supposed to cross, and then you blame a marshal for not treating the boys with kid gloves. It wasn't Cap's fault that that trail herd got jumped."

"That's the point. It was."

They stared at each other.

"That's what I'm trying to tell you," Warner said. "Cap was killed, not in the line of duty, but at Mary Hoolian's place. He'd gone there to meet the men who rustled that herd. There was a thousand dollars in his pocket when Doc and I searched his body. Apparently he and the men he was working with quarreled over the payoff."

Condon looked slowly around the ring of watching faces. It seemed impossible that these men, who had known Cap Lennox for two years, could actually believe this silly charge. Cap Lennox had been a hard man, living in a hard world, but there had been no dishonesty in him.

But their expressions showed that each and every one believed with Warner.

"So you see," Lloyd Warner said, "why we hesitated before we appointed you to fill Cap's place. We were fairly certain that you hadn't been in on any of Cap's deals. We don't know who he was working with, but the streets below the railroad are filled with gamblers and sharpers and loose women."

Condon had gained control of his anger. He said ironically, "Want them cleaned out?"

He saw shock run through them, and hid his secret smile. Of course they did not want them cleaned out. Men off the trail demanded entertainment and they preferred it raw. What these city fathers wanted was the business of the trail herds without the trouble of meeting the problems which the riders presented.

He knew that he should follow his first resolve. He should walk out of this room, ride out of this stuffy, self-satisfied town, leaving them to stew in their own trouble. But he also knew that he no longer could.

Cap Lennox had taken no crooked money, and Joe Condon meant to stay here until he proved it.

He stood silent as the mayor pinned the star upon his shirt, and listened to the small man make his little speech.

Chapter Three

It was dark when he came down the three steps, but not so dark that he failed to catch movement beside the gate of the neat picket fence.

He stopped. He dropped his hand on the stock of his heavy gun. "Speak up," he said. "Who's there?"

Light laughter reached him, and then Lucy's amused voice. "I didn't mean to startle the marshal."

He smiled under the cover of the darkness, finding her laughter infectious, and moved down the walk. She was leaning against the gate.

"I wanted to congratulate you," she said. "Papa is old-fashioned in many ways. He doesn't believe a woman should be included when men hold meetings."

He hesitated, the amusement gone. "Would it surprise you to know that I entered the house with the full intention of resigning and leaving the Springs?"

He could not see her face clearly in the shadow, but her tone showed that he had surprised her. "Leaving? Was it the girl we met on the train?"

Suddenly he wanted to tell her that Kern Alder no longer meant anything to him; that he had fled from her once, but in the year of absence he had measured her fairly and found her lacking. No, it was not Kern he was running from now, but Lucy herself, Lucy and the knowledge that she never could be for him. But he could not tell her. She was too kind to take pleasure in the fact that more than one man wanted her.

Instead he said, "It wasn't Kern," and dismissed her by his tone. "With Cap dead I simply had no interest in staying, but now it's different. Those fools in there think he was killed because he was a thief."

She said in a tentative voice, "My father showed me the money."

"What does money prove?" he said harshly. "Was it marked? Do they know where it came from? I wouldn't believe Cap guilty if I saw him steal those cows with my own eyes."

"Then what—why was he killed?"

"I don't know, but I'm going to find out, and God help the ones who are responsible when I do. Cap had one thing he was proud of—his honor, his reputation. He ran the best trail town in Kansas. We had less trouble here, less bloodshed. But he was in someone's way."

She said impulsively, "I like loyalty," and reached out to touch his hand. "Be careful."

He took the memory of those words through the gate and along the wooden sidewalk toward Railroad Avenue.

The wall bracket lamp was burning in the

marshal's office when he came in. Blankton still lounged at the desk and Phil Moore seemed not to have moved.

They watched him without change of expression, waiting for him to speak. He didn't speak. He crossed to the desk and stood there until Blankton lifted himself from the chair and stepped aside so that he could sit down.

He pulled out the drawers, one after another, removing Cap's personal things. They watched him stack them into a neat pile. Finally Blankton could stand the suspense no longer.

"Did you resign?"

"I did not."

The man sneered. "I didn't expect you to. I knew all you wanted was to be coaxed."

Condon's eyes had been on the pitifully small pile of Cap's belongings. He lifted them to meet Blankton's.

"There's no reason in the world why I should account to you for my actions," he said roughly, "but I'm going to. I went over to Warner's fully intending to resign, and they told me a fantastic tale about Cap playing in with rustlers, about his falling out with them and getting himself shot."

Blankton said, "What's that got to do with you turning in your badge?"

"Cap stole nothing in his whole life," Condon said. "You know it as well as I do. I'd be a dirty dog to walk out now, leaving the town to think him a thief."

Blankton laughed. "You make it sound like a Sunday school. This is one of the toughest towns in Kansas. Cap knew it and he knew the chances he took wearing the star. What the hell. I don't know whether he helped steal those cattle or not. All I know is that he rousted the crew, because I helped him. Maybe one of them sneaked into Mary's and shot him and planted the money in his pocket. Maybe it was old man Warner himself. Warner was sore about the way Cap manhandled those Texans. The old bastard is afraid that the other herds heading north will hear what happened and drive back to Dodge. Anyhow, if Cap didn't have his hand out it was his own damn fault. A man doesn't get paid enough in this job anyway."

Condon stared up at Blankton, at the man's veiled, wicked eyes. "I should turn in the badge," he said, "and leave you to run the town. It's what the fatheads north of Railroad Avenue deserve, and what you deserve. You'd be dead in two weeks."

He stood up slowly, his hand going to the buckle of his sagging gunbelt. "Take off your gun," he said.

Blankton gaped at him.

"Take off your gun. I'm going to beat some sense into your hard head."

Suddenly a savage eagerness lighted Blankton's narrow face. He reached down with his left hand and unbuckled his belt, saying, "You make a mistake this time, Joseph, my boy. I've been wanting to get my hands on you ever since you blew into town. I don't like smart kids and I hate Texans."

He handed his gunbelt to Phil Moore, and a look passed between them. Condon saw it and realized that Moore was almost as hungry to see him beaten as Blankton was. They both hated him because Cap had treated him as an equal while he barely tolerated them.

He put his own gun on the top of the scarred desk and stepped around it, standing relaxed, waiting. He did not wait long. Blankton charged, aiming a looping right at his head. Condon ducked under the blow, caught a left to the forehead and drove his own right hand hard into Blankton's body.

He heard the man grunt and saw him step back. He followed, hooked a left to the head, and buried a right in the stomach which drove Blankton back against the wall with a jar that shook the office.

The man stood there, his shoulders against the rough boards, his mouth half open as he tried to drink enough air to replace that which had been driven from his big body. His eyes were partly glazed as he stared at Condon.

Then he gained new strength and gathered

himself. He charged again, head down like a battering ram which ignored the blows Condon pounded against him. He broke through, his shoulder hitting Condon squarely in the stomach, his powerful arms wrapping about the lighter man's ribs, carrying him to the floor.

They crashed down, Blankton on top, the force of the impact seeming almost to collapse Condon's ribs. He rolled, and they went over and over together until Condon's head cracked hard against one of the desk legs.

The jar did not knock him out, but it fuddled his senses and he lost his grip. Blankton shook free and struggled to his feet, using the edge of the desk as a kind of ladder to drag himself up.

Condon's gun lay on desk, only inches from Blankton's hand. He reached out, shook it loose from the holster and twisted, intending to bring the heavy barrel down on Condon's head.

But as Blankton turned, Joe Condon scrambled to his knees and wrapped his arms around Blankton's legs, tackling him, carrying him back down to the floor. In the fall Blankton lost his hold on the gun and it slid away from them to Phil Moore's feet.

Phil stooped to pick it up, his eyes glittering a little as he weighed the weapon in his hands, watching the fighters thrashing across the floor.

Blankton broke free again and fought to his feet. This time Condon came up with him. They stood for a moment facing each other, panting as their lungs struggled for air, and then Condon moved in.

He stalked his man, deliberately, on balance, ready. He took a swinging left to the head without even trying to guard against the blow, and drove his left into Blankton's side. Then he buried his right under the man's heart.

It was like cutting at a tree with a sharp axe. No single blow put Blankton down, but each impact from the hard fists weakened the man. He still fought back, wildly, desperately, without thought, without even clear understanding, but to the watching Phil Moore it was now apparent that Blankton stood no chance of winning.

Condon's face was battered, of course. One eye was puffed. He had a small cut at the corner of his mouth and a deep bruise near his left ear. But he kept boring in. There was something cruelly machine-like in his motions, as if he didn't feel pain, as if nothing Blankton could do would stop him.

Blankton sensed this. His blows became wilder, driven by despair, but the heart seemed to go out of him. And then Condon, who had been directing most of his attention to the body, suddenly shifted his attack to the head. He sent over a left to the cheek and then a short, looping right uppercut which crashed against Blankton's jaw.

Blankton sat down. He landed close to the desk,

so that his back rested against the corner. But then he slowly twisted sidewise, and slid rather than fell, until his shoulder and cheek lay against the dirty floor.

Joe Condon stared down at him in a kind of numbed surprise. From the moment his head had cracked against the desk leg, he had been only half conscious, fighting more from the instinct to survive than from plan.

He turned groggily, using the back of his hand to wipe away the blood which leaked from the cut beside his mouth, and he saw Phil Moore standing against the window, holding Condon's gun loosely in his hand.

Understanding came to Condon, clearing the tiredness which fogged his brain. "Give me that," he said.

Phil Moore flinched visibly. He shoved the gun away from him, holding it at arm's length yet not pointing it at anything. His tone was not quite steady as he said, "He dropped it. I just picked it up. I—"

Condon held out his hand. Phil Moore reversed the gun and put it into Condon's palm.

"Joe, I—" His mouth seemed to be too dry, and he kept looking away as if he did not want to see Blankton's long body huddled on the floor.

Condon stepped to the desk, picked up his belt and buckled it around his flat hips. He examined the gun and slid it into its place in the holster.

Then he fixed Moore with eyes which held no mercy.

"Phil, a man who wants to do something and lacks the nerve isn't worth a damn."

For an instant Phil Moore's nostrils flared, but then he got himself under control. "I don't know what you mean," he said.

"Don't you?" Joe Condon said. "Just remember this. Never get behind me on a dark street."

Blankton stirred and groaned and sat up. For a while he did nothing but sit, feeling his jaw, looking into space as minutes ticked by. Finally he dragged himself upward and slumped against the edge of the desk.

Condon watched him without expression. Blankton shook his head and spat on the floor, his spittle laced with blood from his cut lip. His eyes were clearing, and Condon had time to wonder at a thing which had astonished him before—the ability of a man to take a thorough beating and yet recuperate within minutes.

Blankton shook his head again. His eyes shed their glaze of shock, became completely functional. They watched Condon now with an awareness which held neither anger nor liking.

"You licked me." He ran one hand across his face as if trying to wipe away the knowledge. "You licked me."

Condon said nothing.

Blankton's voice turned bitter. "You're half

Indian, Joe. I always knew it. No one ever licked me before."

Still Condon didn't speak. He waited.

Blankton wiped his mouth and spat again. "I suppose I'm through?"

"Not unless you want it that way."

Surprise made Blankton blink and stare at the man he had been trying to kill only a few short minutes before. "I don't get it," he said.

"Don't you?" said Joe. "Well, make no mistake. I don't like you. I never have. But supposing I lifted your badge. You wouldn't leave town."

Blankton shook his head. "Probably not."

"All right," Condon said. "If you're going to stay you might as well wear the badge. I know you, and you know me, and you're a good hand when you want to be."

He could see that Blankton was thinking it over. He did not add that he did not want Blankton or anybody else who might be useful to leave until he found Cap Lennox's murderer. He turned and walked to the door, conscious that both men watched him. He did not glance around. He opened the door quietly, stepped out into the night, and closed the door behind him.

He stayed motionless for a full minute, listening, but no sound of voices came through the thin boards. He moved on, smiling a little mirthless smile as he headed up the sidewalk toward the hotel.

Chapter Four

The hotel lobby was deserted when he entered it, and sound from the dining room to the right indicated that most of the tenants were occupied with the evening meal.

He walked the length of the narrow lobby, rounded the desk and took his key from the hook on the board. Then he climbed the stairs and went along the upper hall to his room.

This, he thought wryly as he lighted the lamp and looked around the cell-like space, was home. The paper had once had a rose pattern, but the careless actions of a hundred tenants had smudged it until the print was hard to distinguish from the dirt spots.

The enamel which had coated the iron bedstead was chipped and stained and the mattress sagged to a depression in the middle as though a buffalo had wallowed in it.

He stripped, tossing his soiled and bloody clothes in a pile at the foot of the bed. Then, standing naked, he poured water from the pitcher into the bowl and sponged the grime from his body.

Afterward, he stepped before the clouded mirror and examined the marks which the fight had left upon his face.

The eye was swollen, but he guessed it would not close. The cut at the corner of his mouth had ceased to bleed, and he felt surprisingly well despite the battering he had taken. He dressed, thankful for the clean clothes, and ran a comb through his still damp hair, plastering it in an effort to iron out its natural curl.

Finished, he put his hat in place, buckled the gunbelt about his flat hips and went back downstairs. The lobby was half full of people, and more were coming from the big dining room.

He spoke to several, nodded to others and saw curiosity awaken as they noted his bruises. But it was characteristic that none felt close enough to him to comment on the marks.

This was something he had cultivated almost from the first moment he had pinned on the deputy's star—an aloofness which held him from close friendship with any man in town. And now that he had moved up into the marshal's place, he meant to continue it. He turned into the dining room and chose one of the small tables against the wall, ignoring the large center one which was still littered with the debris of the evening meal.

Clara Calhoun came to serve him. She was a large girl in her plain wash dress, handsome rather than pretty, with a certain boldness of manner which had been heightened by long service in the hotel dining room.

"Well, look at you!" She grinned as she set the butter and sourdough bread upon the table. "What have you been trying to do, plow up our main street with your nose?"

He gave her a brief smile in return. Of all the people who worked around the hotel he liked her best. She was a ranch girl whose family had broken apart at her mother's death, and she had drifted from one railhead camp to another until she finally settled in the Springs.

She would bandy words with the drummers, the cattle buyers and the ranchers who came to the hotel, but Condon, who knew more of the morals of the town's citizens than anyone else, had never seen her in the company of a man.

He said, "You should see the other fellow."

Her grin widened. "They all say that. I never in my life found a man who would admit he'd got licked. Somebody has to lose a fight once in a while. They can't all be Mexican stand-offs."

"In that country the loser usually gets buried," he told her soberly.

Her eyes darkened and the smile went away from her generous mouth, leaving it somewhat grim. "I'm sorry about Cap," she said so softly that the words were almost lost in the clatter from the kitchen. "He was all right. I watched him for two years and a woman alone can usually size up a man. She has to." She walked away and disappeared through the kitchen door, and then a voice behind him said, "You don't care where you find your women, do you?"

He turned to find Kern Alder watching him, her green eyes unreadable, the slightly mocking smile curving her full lips. She came around to sit down facing him, her elbows on the table, her small chin caught in the cup of her hands.

He studied her, remembering the power she had had to hurt him, surprised to find that it was entirely gone. "Kern," he said, "it's no good. I danced to your tune for three years, but that time is gone."

Her eyes changed a little.

"Who is it—the other girl?"

He smiled at her then. "Why is it when a woman loses her power over a man she immediately thinks of another woman? Maybe I just saw through your games. Maybe I just got tired playing the part of a dancing bear."

"You were a man once," she said half angrily. "Now I find you hiding behind a tin star."

"Kern, how many things have you wanted in your life that you couldn't get?"

"Very few."

"You had me," he said, "halter broke and ready to come on call. And then you decided that you wanted Rick."

"That was a mistake, Joe."

"Because he wouldn't stand hitched for all your fancies?"

"I knew I'd made a mistake as soon as you were out of sight of the house," she said, very serious now. "I expected you back in the fall. I nearly died when you didn't come home, when the boys said you'd stayed behind. Why do you think I'm here now?"

Once he would have given his hope of heaven to believe her. Now it shocked him to find that he did not care. All that had passed between them seemed to have been washed away.

She took his silence for hesitation. "Listen to me, Joe Condon. I never chased a man before in my life."

"Not unless it suited your purpose."

"Be nasty. I deserve it. But don't be a damn fool. What future do you have as a marshal, a dog, taking orders from lesser men?"

Her understanding surprised him. "I was going to quit tonight," he said, and because Kern Alder for all her faults was anything but a fool, he went on to tell her what the town council had said about Cap Lennox, and what Cap had meant to him. It was a relief to have her to talk to. They were bound by years of association, of memories in common. He told her about the town, about its divided loyalties, about the senseless charge that Cap had helped steal cattle from the trail herd.

She listened well, giving his words her full attention. She was a different person when her emotions were not affected. She had her father's hardness, and his shrewdness.

"You're a fool," she said finally. "What good can you do Lennox now that he's dead? You can't win. The foreman of the herd that was raided is still at the hotel. I talked with him a while ago. He swears he'll stay in town until he finds out who stole his cows."

"I want to talk to him."

"Don't worry," she said with more grimness than she intended. "He'll talk to you." She waited until he finished his meal and then she led him out into the lobby.

The foreman, Howe, was a big man with a taut, sunburned face and hard, restless eyes. He stood silently sizing Condon up while Kern introduced them, then said in his soft, slurring voice, "Miss Kern says you're all right, that you're a Texan who rode for her father."

Condon nodded. He understood Howe. He had known a hundred like him, soft-spoken yet explosive, dangerous when aroused.

"I wasn't here when you got raided, Howe. Can you tell us what happened?"

Howe stared at the badge on Condon's shirt as if the star were something he intensely disliked. "We were camped about twenty miles south," he said. "It was a dark night. They hit us and stampeded the bunch. We were too busy trying to stop the cattle to pay much attention to anything else. The next afternoon we finally got them rounded up and drove on to the pens. We were over five hundred short on the tally."

Condon might have asked: Are you certain you didn't just lose that many in rounding up the herd? Are you sure that the stampede wasn't started by natural causes, maybe lightning?

But he didn't. He knew his man. Howe was not the type to make a mistake like that.

He said, "Did you search for them? Pick up any tracks?"

"You're damn right we did. We picked up their tracks three days later. We also picked up tracks where half a dozen riders cut away from the herd and headed back to town. The men who made that raid are here." It was a challenge, thrown directly at Condon. "And your boss led them," Howe added.

Condon did not deny it. There was no point in picking a fight with Howe.

"And I'll tell you something else." Howe's eyes had begun to glitter. "There's other herds coming up the trail—a lot of them, more cattle than you ever saw before—and there better not be any trouble when they get here. If there is, we'll bunch up and take this town to pieces."

Condon said levelly, "There won't be any trouble. I wasn't here when it happened. But I'll tell you one thing now—Cap Lennox had no part in it."

"Then why was he killed?"

"Maybe you killed him," Condon said softly.

Howe bristled. "When I kill a man it's on the street and he has a gun in his hand." He turned and stalked from the hotel.

Kern Alder said, "That wasn't wise. You made an enemy of him. He would be much better as a friend."

Suddenly Joe Condon felt harried. Trouble was building up on all sides of him, and he had no one to turn to for advice, no one to offer help.

He left Kern with barely a word, and headed for the marshal's office. Blankton sat slumped in the chair behind the desk. He had washed and changed his clothes, but the marks of battle were still on him. Also, for the first time since Joe Condon had known him, Blankton showed a trace of embarrassment.

"Where's Phil?" Condon asked.

"On the street. He took my patrol tonight. I thought the more I kept out of sight the less the tongues would wag."

"Let them wag," Condon said. "Maybe it will make them stop talking about Cap. What do you know about this Howe?"

"He's a trouble-maker. He talked big, and his boys got drunk, and Cap and I threw them in jail. He swore to kill us both. Now he's offered a thousand-dollar reward to anybody who can point out the rustlers and he's sitting around waiting for results."

"No takers?"

"None that I know of."

"What else is new?"

Blankton shrugged and indicated a sheaf of reward dodgers on a corner of the desk. "Those came. The jail's empty. We had three drunks last night but I turned them loose this morning. I guess the town was so shocked by Cap's death that everybody's behaving himself."

Condon said thoughtfully, "We'll need another deputy. Got any ideas?"

Blankton looked startled, then said with elaborate carelessness, "That's up to you."

"What about your brother?"

This time Blankton could not keep the surprise out of his voice. "I don't get you, Joe. You don't like me. I don't think you even trust me. You licked me tonight, and if I'd been in your place I'd have fired me."

Condon said nothing.

"And now you talk about appointing my kid brother. Why don't you appoint one of your friends?"

"I have no friends," Condon told him. "If I did have I wouldn't want one for a deputy. I don't want a friend working for me."

Blankton rubbed his chin. "Maybe that makes sense."

Condon did not try to explain. He said, "Talk to the kid. It will pay one seventy-five and he'll have the midnight-to-morning trick. I'm going to shift Phil over to days. He'll take over until two. You work from noon until midnight, and I'll double with all of you as I'm needed."

Blankton made no answer and Condon expected none. He said, "Tonight you bunk down here in case you're needed. I'll send Phil to bed at midnight."

Blankton said, "You're the one who needs sleep." It was the first time in their association that he had ever shown any concern for Condon's comfort.

Condon shrugged and left the office. He walked along Denver Street to the corner of First, and in the light cast from a store window he recognized two approaching figures as the mayor and Lloyd Warner. He stopped and they saw him.

"Good evening, Marshal," Warner said jovially. "We were just coming along to the office to have a talk with you."

He said, "Blankton's there."

Warner hesitated for the barest instant. "Then we'd better have our little talk here. I don't care to mention it before all the members of the council, but Mary Hoolian has to go."

Condon had not given it thought, but he was not surprised. Mary Hoolian and her kind operated by sufferance, and Mary had broken the cardinal, unwritten rule. She had let bad trouble start in her place. Cap Lennox had been killed there.

That the woman probably had nothing to do with Cap's death was beside the point. She would have to go. Public opinion would not permit her to continue her operations. Condon felt no real sorrow for Mary. She was in a hard business, and she understood as well as he did that the rule had been broken. She would move on to one of the new railhead towns, taking those of her girls who would go with her.

"It should be handled quietly," Warner said. "If she gets difficult we'll have to raid her of course, but for all concerned it would be better if she merely shuts her door and fades out of town."

Joe Condon understood him. If they were forced to raid the house and jail some of the girls, it would call attention to the fact that certain things contrary to town ordinances were tolerated because of the trail herd crews. Everyone in the Springs knew that places like Mary's existed there, but no one north of the tracks ever discussed it, especially in mixed company.

"I'll take care of it," he said. "I know Mary. There will be no trouble. She understands."

He could see the relief on their faces, even in the uncertain light, and he knew they felt better about his appointment now. Neither Warner nor Boyce would have relished the job of crossing the tracks and carrying the message to Mary, but they felt no compunction at handing the job to him.

Lloyd Warner nodded, and the mayor murmured something which could have been thanks but was not. Then they marched back up First toward the warmth and security of their homes, a security which now rested neatly on Condon's shoulders.

He watched them go. He made a right turn into First and followed it, crossing Railroad Avenue and pausing to look along the boardwalk which ran past the lighted saloons. The street was nearly devoid of life. A few ponies stood hip-shot at the long rails, waiting with sleepy patience for their riders.

A knot of men, perhaps a dozen, stood beside the entrance of one of the lesser saloons a block away. Condon studied them with practiced attention, deciding by trained instinct that there was no trouble here.

He moved to the corner swinging door which gave entrance to the Western Belle and glanced over the louvred doors at the smoky room beyond. It was only half full and the crowd around the gambling tables at the rear seemed orderly, almost subdued.

Satisfied, he followed First southward for two blocks until it ended in a maze of narrow streets little better than alleys. Turning left, he tramped along the muddy track, avoiding as best he could the puddles which made walking hazardous.

Before a two-storied house which towered above its surrounding shacks he stopped and stood for an instant, studying the lighted windows which sent their glow across the low porch. Then he climbed the two steps, crossed the painted boards and tried the door. It was locked.

Never in his seven months in the town had this door been locked. He hesitated, then knocked on the glass panel which formed the upper half of the door. Beyond the glass there were heavy red curtains, so heavy that only a little light came through, casting a crimson glow across the porch.

The bolt clicked and slid discreetly. The door opened a crack and he had a view of a pale face and pale gold hair.

"We're not open."

He said, "It's Joe Condon," in a tone of quiet authority. The door opened wide. The girl stepped aside.

"I guess you can come in," she said. "I guess even Mary can't keep the law out."

Chapter Five

Condon stepped into the square hall and paused to watch the girl bolt the door. She was young, with a certain prettiness not yet entirely marred by the hard lines which were forming about her mouth. Her hair was pale, her eyes a deep blue, and he thought fleetingly that given a better set of circumstances she could have been beautiful.

She turned to find his gaze upon her, and she met it with a kind of stubborn aggressiveness, as if she dared him to offer criticism of any kind.

He said, "Evening, Flora. I've got to see Mary."

"Are we going to have to move?"

He did not answer her. Instead he said, "Mary in her room?"

She nodded and he moved forward to climb the stairs which ran up against one of the hall's papered walls.

At the top he came about and followed the corridor to the front of the house. He knocked on the closed door. A muffled voice came through the panel. "Who is it?"

"Joe Condon."

After a marked delay, the voice said, "Come in, Joe," and he pushed open the door.

Mary Hoolian sat in a red plush rocker beside the front window. From the window could be seen the full crazy-quilt pattern of the twisting alleys as they ran out to lose themselves in the rolling hills which bordered the town.

She was a large woman, not quite middle-aged, with a humorous mouth and the coolest eyes he had ever encountered. But the eyes had changed. Tonight they looked haunted, and he realized with a shock that Mary was scared.

He had seen her many times, in a number of different circumstances, but he had never seen her scared before.

That she and Cap had been on friendly terms was no secret; but then, Cap had been on speaking terms with every woman along the row.

She said, "Have you come to move us out?" and she actually sounded hopeless.

"I'm more interested in who killed Cap and why, Mary."

"I don't know, Joe. He was talking to some men in the back room. I didn't see any of them except Cap."

"You're lying, Mary. You know more about what goes on in this town than Cap ever did."

Her mouth shut, trap-like. She stared at him, her face utterly bleak.

"Cap was a friend of yours."

Her laugh was as harsh and mirthless as the cawing of a crow. "A friend. What is a friend? There are two types of people who have no friends, Joe. Marshals and whores. I don't know who killed Cap or why. Maybe Pete Ortman knows. Go to the Western Belle and talk to Pete."

He felt a sudden tensing of the muscles across his back. "Are you trying to say that Pete killed Cap?"

"Hell no. Pete was the best friend he had, about the only friend he had. If anyone knows what's happening in this town it's Pete. But Pete's like me. He wants to stay in business. He wants to stay alive."

He felt as if he had come up against a blank wall. He sensed that Mary had the information he wished, but that he could say nothing which would make her tell him. He tried anyway.

"They're running you out," he said. "You're protecting somebody and whoever he is, he's standing aside and offering no help. Help me, Mary, and I'll try to help you."

She shook her head. "No soap, Joe. Just watch yourself. No one can help me, but I learned a long time ago to keep my mouth shut about what I see and hear. It's the only way you can hope to stay alive in this business. We'll be on the first train west in the morning."

He said, "Is there anything I can do to help? The house—are you going to sell it?"

"Pete Ortman will take care of it. There's nothing. We'll probably never see each other again." She did not rise, and did not offer her hand. He stopped beside the door, trying to think of something to say. Failing, he left her.

Flora was waiting for him in the lower hall, her light hair like a crown around her small face. She said in a low voice, "We can't go out on the street, and we're leaving early in the morning. I've got to get him a note. He won't know where I went."

"Who won't?"

She hesitated. "Sam Seller."

A picture of the tired woman with the three exhausted children he had seen on the train rose to Condon's mind. He frowned.

Flora mistook the frown and put out one slim hand to grip his arm. The other held a folded sheet of paper. "Please, Marshal. There's no one else I can ask. Get him the note. He can't come here. Mary wouldn't let him in, but he could be at the station in the morning."

Her eyes were big, shiny with tears she had forgotten how to shed. Out of his own loneliness there rose a sympathy for her, and he silently extended his hand. She put the folded sheet into his palm, then pulled back the bolt and opened the door. He stepped out into the night.

The chill air was like a bracing drink after the overheated perfume of the upper room, and he paused at the edge of the porch to fill his lungs.

A man came down the street, weaving a little, singing in an off-key undertone to himself. He turned into an alley. Condon watched him reflectively until he vanished into the darkness, then moved down into the muddy street and plodded toward Railroad Avenue, carrying Flora's note in his hand.

He had no desire to play God. It was none of his business if Sam Seller wanted to make a fool of himself over Flora. But the memory of the woman and the children on the train still troubled him.

He supposed that with Flora gone, Seller would find another girl. The man was no good and never would be. His wife and children would probably be better off without him.

Unconsciously he closed his hand, crumpling Flora's note into a wadded ball. Then he dropped it into the mud and stepped upon it, twisting in a pivoting motion until it was buried deeply in the mire.

Afterward he went on, but he knew that for days he would be haunted by the pleading he had seen in Flora's eyes. He swore softly under his breath, shrugging, as if he might shake away the feeling of guilt by the gesture.

Flora would be better off too. A man like Seller would never bring her help. Condon did not know, but he suspected that the gambler had not been above taking part of the girl's pitiful earnings.

He walked faster as he neared the end of the

board sidewalk. He reached the corner and paused, checking Railroad Avenue carefully before turning into it. He saw a small group of men a quarter of a block away.

They stood in a patch of light thrown by a saloon window, clearly silhouetted. He counted four of them—three standing in a kind of triangle around a fourth man. The man in the middle was Phil Moore, and it was obvious to Condon's experienced eye that Moore had made the usually fatal mistake of letting someone get behind him. They had him whipsawed.

Two of the men were half drunk, and Condon had never seen them before. The third was Howe, the trail herd foreman. Howe stood directly before Moore, his voice carrying along the street. "We've been waiting a chance to catch you alone, Deputy. Who were the men that helped your boss steal our cattle?"

Moore stood with his hands swinging at his sides, fidgeting like a baffled cat surrounded by hungry dogs. He knew that whatever happened he would get a bullet in the back, and fear showed all over him.

"I don't know," he said. "I didn't have anything to do with it."

Howe was enjoying himself. "Talk up," he said, "or we'll show this town what Texas does to cow thieves. We'll hang you to the nearest tree, lawman."

Even as he came round the corner Condon knew what he would do. He did not touch his gun. A shot might bring one of Howe's men down, but it would certainly mean Moore's death.

He came forward as quietly as he could, close to the dark store fronts. He was within ten feet of them when Moore said desperately, "I wasn't close to Cap. Ask Joe Condon."

"Ask me," Condon said. He covered the last ten feet in three running steps, hitting Howe's back with the point of his shoulder, knocking him sidewise across the hitch rail and into the dust of the street, never breaking stride as he plunged forward to catch the second man, driving him hard against the post beside the saloon doorway.

The third rider, caught flat-footed, grunted in disbelief and clawed at his gun. Then Phil Moore came to life, springing in and carrying the man down to the dirty sidewalk.

Howe had fallen on his shoulder. He rolled, coming up with the quickness of a cat. But he was not fast enough. Condon spun around, drawing as he turned. His bullet kicked the half-raised gun from Howe's fingers.

For an instant the trail foreman stared at his empty hand as if he could not believe his senses. Slowly his eyes came up to meet Condon's and he spat the gritty dust of the street from his lips.

"You renegade," he said. "Fighting Texans for a bunch of damyankees!"

Condon said coldly, "I don't need two helpers to jump one man." He stepped back so that he could cover the Texan he had driven against the hotel door post. The man was just climbing to his knees.

"Careful how you come up," Condon said, and realized that a crowd was forming about them, attracted by the sound of the fight. "All right, Phil."

Phil Moore had gotten the gun of the man who lay under him. He rose with it in his hand and disarmed the rider who stood now beside the saloon window, shaking his head as if to clear it, the liquor driven out of him.

Howe ducked under the rail and stepped up on the sidewalk. "We aren't through, Marshal."

"You're all through in this town," Condon said. "I've got other things on my mind than fighting the war over again along Railroad Avenue. Get your horses and ride out. If I find you in town an hour from now I'll slam you in jail and keep you there."

Howe sucked in a ragged, raging breath. "A man gets robbed," he said. "And then he gets thrown in jail for trying to get back his stock."

"For trying to take things in his own hands," Condon corrected him. "I'll try to get back your steers. I hate a cow thief as much as you do. But no one carries guns in my town, and no one talks about hanging. Now get out."

"Our guns."

Condon looked at his hot eyes. "Give me your address. I'll ship them back to Texas."

Someone in the crowd laughed. Howe swore under his breath. "We'll be back, Condon, with the first herd up the trail. We'll burn the goddam stinking town to the ground." He turned on his heel, striding away. His riders followed him.

Phil Moore said haltingly, "Thanks Joe."

Condon turned to look at him. "Damn a man who doesn't stand up for his own." He walked away, carrying the captured guns, pushing his way through the crowd toward the Western Belle.

Chapter Six

He came into the saloon, laying the guns on the bar, saying, "I don't think they'll be after them." He gave the long room a careful scrutiny, knowing that everyone in the place was watching him, and then he moved toward the rear where eight poker tables made a kind of cluster. Six of them were occupied, but the one Cap Lennox had always used and the one next to it were vacant.

He herded his way forward, around Cap's old table, and settled into a chair that put his back flush against the rear wall. This chair had belonged to Cap. Never occupied by anyone else, it had been a kind of throne from which he ruled the town. Cap had spent many more hours in it than he had spent in the marshal's office.

He had once explained this to Condon. "A peace officer," he'd said, "should be seen, and his badge should be in plain sight so that strangers will not mistake him. By his very presence he can often halt trouble before it really gets started."

The room had been fairly quiet as Condon came in, and the attention of everyone in it had centered on him. Now as he settled into the seat a wave of sound rose as if the men had been holding their breaths to see what he would do, and his action in taking Cap Lennox's old seat was a kind of answer. The king was dead, long live the king.

A dozen men crowded forward, some shaking his hand, others merely telling him that they were glad he had the job. He answered them unsmilingly, nodding mostly, without words. He knew he could make himself popular here merely by ordering a round of drinks, but he had no desire for their friendship, no desire for any man's friendship that could be purchased across a bar. Nor did he have the ease of manner which had made Cap Lennox universally accepted.

They drifted away finally, leaving Pete Ortman standing alone beside the table. The saloon owner turned, letting his quick eyes range about the room. Then he took the empty chair on Condon's right, hitching it around until their shoulders nearly touched.

"Drink?"

Condon refused the offer. He examined the saloon man openly, studying him with care, as if he had never seen him before.

Pete Ortman was not young by frontier standards. Most men who had chosen to try their luck in the railroad towns were well under forty, but if Condon was any judge Ortman was well into his fifties.

He was a solid man, just under six feet, with powerful shoulders and arms which seemed a little too long for the rest of him. He had fair skin and a round head and soft, fluffy auburn hair, just beginning to gray at the temples. His mustache was full, silky and flowing and his brown eyes had a deceptive mildness. As Condon well knew, this was not a soft or mild man.

He had followed the rail camps westward, housing his saloon in one tent after another until he struck Dexter. Here he had stayed, building the Western Belle, serving as a kind of unofficial mayor for the people south of the tracks.

Ortman said with a slight smile, "Trying to make me look like one of the pictures on a reward dodger, Marshal?"

Joe Condon shook his head. At the moment he felt very young and inexperienced, knowing that the man who faced him was shrewd and in many ways ruthless. "I was wondering how honest you are, Pete."

The words surprised Ortman. It showed in the flickering of the eyes, but after his first reaction his smooth mask dropped back into place, leaving his heavy face bland and unreadable.

"As honest as necessary," he said in a slightly mocking voice. "As honest as necessary."

"You think I'm pretty young?" Condon said. "Pretty green?"

The mockery disappeared from Ortman's eyes and his voice sharpened a little when he answered. "You've surprised me twice in the last three minutes, Joe. I've watched you ever since you came here. It's part of my business to watch people, to know people, to understand what makes them tick. I thought Cap was crazy when he hired you, but I'm beginning to change my mind. You've learned a lot. Maybe you've learned enough to wear that badge and still manage to stay alive."

"Cap didn't."

Ortman sighed. "The percentages catch up with a man sooner or later. I've known Cap for five years. I saw him in some tough places and I saw him come out with a whole skin. This time he missed."

Condon looked out over the big room. The place was beginning to fill up. Customers stood two deep before the bar. Every chair at every poker table except this one was occupied, and every game had its standee audience, watching the play.

But no one seemed to be paying any attention to this table. No one seemed surprised that he sat there, conferring with Ortman, and he remembered suddenly that Ortman had sat thus with Cap, night after night. He had never given it much thought before.

But if association meant anything, Ortman had been as good a friend as Cap had. He said abruptly, "I'm going to tell you something. When I heard Cap was dead my first impulse was to turn in the badge and ride on. Cap was the only reason I've stayed in the Springs as long as I have."

Ortman did not answer. He was staring at his hands, which lay soft and idle on the table before him. Joe Condon breathed deeply and then went on. "I was called to Lloyd Warner's tonight. I meant to resign—and then they told me the story about Cap being tied in with the cattle rustlers."

Ortman looked up. "So you decided to stay. You're going to clear Cap's name." He sounded slightly mocking.

"Cap's reputation was all he had. He shouldn't be robbed of it when he's dead."

"Sentiment," the saloon man said. "A marshal has no time for sentiment, boy."

Condon ignored that. He said, "I was at Mary Hoolian's place. She said that if anyone outside of the murderers knew who killed Cap you would be the one."

"She's wrong." There was no hesitation in Ortman's tone. "Mary's known me a long time, and she always figures that I'm smarter than I am."

"She said you were the best friend Cap had."

Ortman seemed to be thinking it over. "Cap and I had some trouble in the first railhead town. Then as the road pushed westward we got to know each other, and we began to trust each other. He let me police the boys south of the tracks. It saved him trouble and made less grief for all of us."

"Is that why he let Mary operate—because you said so?"

"A town like this needs a Mary Hoolian. Her place was orderly and quiet, and she kept her girls off the streets. What more do you want?"

"She has to go. I got the word tonight."

Ortman's eyes darkened. "Where'd the order come from?"

"From the mayor. From Lloyd Warner. Why?"

"Are you sure they thought it up by themselves?"

Condon wasn't. He shook his head. "Why?"

"Let me talk to Mary," Ortman said. "She might answer me when she wouldn't tell you. Cap Lennox never stole a cow or took a crooked dollar in his life, but someone in this town wants us to think he did. The question is, why?"

Condon said with rising impatience, "That's what I've been trying to say to you. If you know something, tell me now."

"I don't," Ortman said. "I know someone stole those cows from Howe, but why should they go to the trouble to discredit Cap? Was he getting too close to their tracks? Were they scared of him?"

"Maybe. Did he say anything to you?"

"Only in a general way. He had the idea that someone big was behind the rustlers. Someone north of the tracks."

Lloyd Warner. The name leaped unbidden into

Condon's mind. The man was a cattle buyer. How simple it would be to drift the stolen animals back to the loading pens, after tallying in the herd. They would become lost in the mass of their original fellow steers. Their road brand would be the same and unless Howe demanded and got a recount, there would be no way of finding out what had happened.

But he dismissed the suspicion almost at once. He could not say he actually liked Lucy's father. The man was too cold, too reserved, too domineering. But to consider him a thief . . . the idea was absurd.

He sat there, feeling a little guilty for even having had the thought. "He gave you no idea?" he asked Condon.

"Cap wasn't much to mention guesses."

"Then if he'd got no closer than that, what possible reason could the thieves have for killing him, for planting that money on his body?"

Ortman said carefully, "Maybe to get rid of me?"

"Meaning?"

"Meaning that they knew Cap would stand behind me, that they could gain nothing by merely killing me—but if Cap were dead and discredited the next marshal might not play along with me."

"But why should they want to get rid of you?"

"I'm guessing." Ortman's tone was studied.

"There's been grumbling among the saloon men and gamblers. They want the town opened up for the coming season. Between us, Cap and I sat on the games. The word went out that if a man was caught cheating he left on the next train. The rule was that if a bartender got caught serving a drunk or feeding him a mickey he hung up his apron. As a result, we didn't have much trouble last season. But the boys are getting hungry. They figure this will be the last big year. Roads are building south of us. The trail herds won't come into Dexter next year."

"So they hope to open up the town?"

"I don't know. I'm guessing."

"Thanks for telling me," Condon said.

"Don't thank me. This is a hard business, and a man looks out for himself when he can. I wasn't going to do anything about Cap's death. You might think I should because we were friends, but Cap would have understood. Everything I have is tied up in this place. I've got to stay here and do business here."

Joe said nothing.

"But this is different," Ortman said. "I'm going to talk to Mary now."

He got up and walked the length of the crowded room and disappeared through the door. Joe Condon raised a finger, caught the bartender's attention and called his order for a beer. Then he turned to watch the card game on his left.

• • •

On the street, Ortman paused to light a cigar. In the flare of the match his features were sharply visible to Hartford Hull who had just come from Talbert's saloon. The newspaper owner saw Ortman turn into the alley, guessed his destination and followed, slipping through the shadows soundlessly, keeping far enough back so that Ortman did not guess that he was being shadowed. Ortman climbed the steps and knocked, but he had to wait several minutes before the door opened for him. Ortman went inside and Hull inched up to a place directly opposite the house, standing in deep shadow, watching the shade which masked the lighted window of Mary Hoolian's room.

He frowned. He did not like loose ends, and Mary was a loose end. None of them knew how much she had guessed. He saw Ortman's silhouette cross back and forth behind the shade. He saw the man's arms gesture and realized that he was arguing. And then, after what seemed hours to the watching man, the light went out. A few minutes later the front door opened. In its oblong of light he saw Ortman and Mary Hoolian, and he heard Mary say in a frightened voice:

"Remember, Pete. If you tell anyone I talked I'll deny every word of it. There's no one else in the world I would have opened my mouth to.

No one. And I wish to God I hadn't told you."

Hartford Hull did not hear Ortman's reply. The door closed. Ortman came down the steps. Hull drew his gun. He raised it, steadying the gun wrist across the crook of his left arm. This time he could not afford to miss. He didn't. The bullet struck Ortman square in the heart.

Hull crept forward to make certain, and then he ran, losing himself in the maze of alleys which converged at the stock pens. He skirted them, crossed the tracks and made his way hastily toward his office.

The shot awakened the south part of town. It was a tribute to the tight rein which Cap Lennox had managed to maintain on the district that gunfire was seldom heard in Dexter Springs.

Joe Condon came away from his table and pushed swiftly through the crowd that was already surging toward the saloon door. He had a horrifying certainty that the victim was Pete Ortman. He had expected the saloon man back a good half-hour ago, and had only lingered in the hope that Ortman might have learned something from Mary.

Men were pouring from the doorways of a dozen saloons, talking excitedly, calling to each other. Joe Condon swung around the corner, running along the alley. He thought himself ahead of the crowd, but as he raced up, a man who had been bending above the body straightened, and with a kind of shock he recognized Phil Moore.

"How'd you get here?" Quick suspicion bristled in his tone, and he heard Moore say in surprise, "I was checking the rear door of Meyer's store. It's only a few hundred feet away."

"See anyone?"

Moore shook his head. Then, as if realizing that Condon might not see the gesture in the darkness, he said, "No one. It's Pete Ortman, dead center."

Condon scarcely glanced at the fallen saloon man. He turned to stare at Mary's house. It was in total darkness. He mounted the steps, heedless of the men who thronged into the alley behind him. He pounded on the door. He thought for a time that there would be no response and debated breaking it down. Then a light showed in the lower hall. The door opened an inch and Mary's scared voice said, "Who is it? What is it?"

"Pete Ortman. He was shot coming down your steps. What did you tell him?"

"Tell him? What do you mean? I haven't seen Pete for a week."

He glared at her, knowing that she was lying, knowing that she knew he knew it, and feeling helpless. How could he make her talk? Did you beat a woman?

"Mary," he said, "Pete was a friend of yours."

She was silent.

"I suppose you didn't even hear the shot?"

"I heard it." She didn't sound so scared now.

"What did you think?"

"I didn't think," she said. "I pulled the covers over my head. It was none of my business."

She closed the door. He heard the bolt shoot into place.

Chapter Seven

The office of the Dexter Springs *Sentinel* was on Denver Street a block and a half east of the hotel. Joe Condon came along the walk, the freshness of the morning lending a spring to his step, and turned into the newspaper doorway to find Hull behind the high counter which separated the front office from the print shop behind it.

Hull was reading proof on a display advertisement. He merely glanced up, smiling as he said, "Be with you in a minute, Joe," and then went back to checking the heavy black smudges left by the 72-point wooden type.

Condon used the interlude to study Hull. The newspaper man was big and his military training had squared his shoulders. His face was pleasing without being handsome, and his light, almost golden hair had a little curl.

The man had magnetism, and since coming to Kansas he had built himself into a position of influence in both state and local affairs.

There could be little doubt that Lucy Warner had chosen well, and yet Condon found that he could not wholly like the man. He thought wryly that perhaps his feeling was born of jealousy, of his knowledge that he loved the girl and had no hope.

Hull looked up suddenly and caught Condon's eyes upon him. A quick, ready smile flashed across his face, which in strict repose had seemed a little sullen.

"Trying to fit me into a wanted dodger, Joe?"

Joe Condon started, and Hull said, "That's what happens when you pin a star on a man. He even begins to suspect his best friends."

Condon's laugh was weak. This was the second time since Cap Lennox's death that Hull had insisted that he and Condon were friends. He said, "It looks as if I'll need all the help I can get, what with Cap and Pete Ortman murdered. Does it strike you as strange that both killings happened at Mary Hoolian's?"

Hull shrugged. "You have to expect violence at a place like Mary's." He studied Condon, his careful machine-like mind analyzing the marshal. "Did you talk to Mary?"

Condon shook his head. "She's scared. She wouldn't open her mouth."

Hull relaxed a little.

"There was something I wanted to ask you," Condon said. "Something that Pete Ortman said before he went out to see Mary last night. He suggested that the man behind these rustlers may live north of the tracks, that he may be a very important person."

"Where," Hartford Hull said slowly, "did he get that idea?"

"I don't know. Maybe from Cap. Maybe it was his own notion."

"Did he say who he thought it was?"

"No." Condon paused. "The first person I thought of was Lloyd Warner."

Hartford Hull had a sudden, almost overpowering desire to laugh. He checked it with difficulty. This was perfect! Nothing could have fitted his purpose better.

"What makes you say that?" he inquired gravely.

"I don't actually believe it can be Warner," Condon told him. "Suspecting him is almost like suspecting you. But it is a logical guess. He's a cattle buyer. He could run the stolen animals back into the pens after the tally and no one would be the wiser."

Hartford Hull pretended to consider. "It makes a kind of sense." He said it grudgingly, and then he smiled. "But Joe, you can't expect me to go along with the idea. After all, Lucy and I are to be married."

"Of course. I shouldn't have mentioned it."

"You should have. A newspaper man is in a strange position. He's supposed to report everything that happens in his paper, but he's also a kind of public conscience. He should help to keep order the same way a marshal does. You don't mind my giving you a piece of advice?"

"That's what I'm here for—partly."

"All right, I'll be perfectly frank with you. I'm responsible for you having the job. The council members were uncertain. They thought you'd been too close to Cap."

Condon said nothing. His poker face bothered Hull a little.

"But I told them I knew you were honest," Hull said. "I told them that whether Cap was mixed up with the cattle thieves or not—which I wasn't convinced of, mind you—I was sure that you weren't."

"Thanks," Condon said, and made it sound dry. He did not like people who reminded him of favors they had done. He thought that perhaps this accounted for some of his reluctance when it came to the matter of accepting Hartford Hull at face value.

"All right," Hull said. "Since I got you appointed, I want you to be a success. None of us likes crime, but we have to remember the kind of town this is, and that men off the long trail need a bit of a fling. I'm not saying that Cap was too strict, but we can't afford to offend the men who bring up the herds."

"That's right."

"I knew you'd understand. After all, you came up with a trail herd yourself. Which reminds me, Lucy said that your girl from Texas was on the train."

"Hardly my girl," Condon said. "She—"

"Lucy said she was pretty. She wants you to bring her to dinner some night."

"I'll try," Joe Condon said, and meant no word of it. He had no desire to go to dinner at the Warner house, or to see Lucy and Kern Alder together. He had been avoiding Kern as much as possible.

He left the office filled with a feeling of unease. He had nothing against Hull, but he could not trust him even though everyone else in town did. All that Hartford Hull said and did seemed exactly right, yet there was something about the man which disturbed him.

And the trouble was, he could not discuss it with anybody in town. He thought of his two deputies and discarded the idea immediately. He could not trust either of them.

He had gone to the newspaper office with the idea of discussing things with Hull, but Hull's cynical attitude had kept him quiet. He even considered going to the bank to talk things over with Lloyd Warner, but dismissed that notion also.

Turning into Second, he walked along it to Railroad Avenue. He reached the corner in time to see a crowd gathering at the station.

He glanced at his watch, then down the track. The westbound was due within a few minutes. As he stood on the corner he saw Mary Hoolian and four of her girls come out of First Street. Mary hesitated, motioned to the Negro roustabout who was pushing a two-wheeled cart piled high with their luggage, and then moved on toward the station.

Condon did not quite know what prompted his next action. Certainly it was not the politic thing to do. The wise thing would be to turn away and go back to Denver Street. Instead he stepped down off the boardwalk and crossed to the station platform.

Coming from the east, he reached it at almost the exact moment that Mary and her girls crossed the tracks and stepped up onto the west end.

The station, a long, low yellow building, ran along the tracks, Railroad Avenue narrowing to alley width to pass north of it. The town resented the arrangement, and there had been talk of forcing the railroad to move the station to the outskirts where the loading pens and freight yards already stood. Nothing had been done about it, however, and as the railroad pointed out, the station and right of way had been there first and the town had grown up around them. In fact, if it came down to cases, the whole width of Railroad Avenue actually belonged to the company and was used as a street only by railroad sufferance.

The platform on either side of the station formed an island, flanked by the two branches of Railroad Avenue, and at the moment this island held a good half hundred people.

Condon sorted his way through them, passing the telegraph bay of the station window and the signal tower, until he came to the thinning edge of the crowd and met Mary Hoolian.

She had dressed as if she were going to a party, cramming her tightly corseted figure into a velvet dress certainly not suitable for traveling, and selecting a saucer shaped hat with a slightly turned-up brim, its flowered decoration standing saucily upright in a mass of ribbon.

Her girls wore quieter garb, and they seemed a little scared. Condon saw Flora looking around the crowd with a kind of hopeless resignation, and realized that she was searching for Sam Seller. A pang of regret went through him. He knew now that he had had no right to destroy her note.

But if the girls were subdued, Mary wasn't. Two men she depended on had been murdered. Now the respectables were forcing her out of town. But she'd be damned if she'd lower her gaudy banner.

She called raucous greetings to male friends in the audience, parading a kind of noisy defiance which caused a shifting in the crowd as the respectable matrons from north of the tracks tried to put the station building between themselves and this menace to their ordered society.

In spite of himself Condon could not quite bury the tiny smile which tugged at the corners of his mouth. For all the cheapness of her display, he saw something almost gallant in the brazen way Mary Hoolian was meeting the world this morning. He wondered if anyone else in the throng realized that her rowdy humor concealed something close to heartbreak.

He saw Warner and the mayor, and guessed by their pained expressions that they were not enjoying the show.

"You're making too much noise, Mary," he said quietly. "Keep it down a little."

She swung to face him, and defiance grew in her bold eyes. This isn't going to be pleasant, he thought. In fact it can get to be pretty nasty.

And then he saw the defiance fade and a deepening sadness take its place. He heard her low-voiced words, almost drowned out as a long-drawn whistle came from the approaching train.

"Sure, Marshal. I don't *feel* like laughing, you know."

He reached out and tucked the fingers of his left hand beneath her elbow and squeezed it reassuringly. She gave him a quick, startled glance and for a moment all the forced gaiety was washed away, leaving her face stark and gaunt and empty. Then her quick smile flashed and she said in an undertone tinged with deep bitterness, "Careful, Marshal. Our betters are watching us."

He said, "Never mind that," and there came the harsh hiss of steam as the train drew in, passing them with a grind of brakes and the steady huffing from its bell stack.

He said, “You’re going away, Mary. Tell me who killed Cap. Tell me who shot Pete on your steps last night.”

But then Mary’s smiling face went blank, expressionless. “I’m not going far enough, Joe. There isn’t a place on this earth far enough.” She turned and climbed the high steps of the coach, showing a length of leg, still nicely turned despite her age.

The girls trouped past him. Flora was the last. She hung back, peering at the crowd as if hoping against hope that Sam Seller would appear. Finally acknowledging defeat, she walked after the others, her eyes puffy with unshed tears.

“He didn’t come,” she said as she passed Joe Condon.

He shook his head. She took one last look, then slid a folded paper into his palm.

“For Sam?”

“For you,” she said, and went quickly up the steps.

He stared after her, struck dumb by surprise. Then he glanced down at the folded slip.

Curiosity prompted him to open it, on the spot, but the Negro in charge of the women’s baggage pushed his cart forward just in time to remind him of a last kindness he could perform. Condon put the note in his shirt pocket. He caught the two top bags and swung up the steps and into the car. Mary Hoolian had established her brood in the two facing seats at the end and was standing in the section across the aisle. He put the bags in the overhead racks and started off after a second load. Mary caught his arm. "Don't come back aboard," she said. "If they get the idea I've talked to you I can't go far enough to be safe."

She pressed a bundle of papers into his hand. "With Ortman dead I have no one I can trust. Here's a power of attorney and a deed. Sell the house for what it will bring and hold the money until you hear from me."

He took them automatically, not knowing what else to do. "Look, Mary, I'll protect you. I'll—"

She laughed, and it was not a pleasant sound. "You're a nice boy, Joe Condon. I've watched you, and I hope you get what you want, although I doubt it. These men are too tough for you, too experienced. Get out while you can—but first, sell my house for what it will bring. I'm not as young as I once was. I can't start over too many more times and this camp is about to blow up."

He tried to ask her what she meant, but the Negro had arrived with the rest of the bags and she pushed him gently out of the way.

The forward door of the coach was behind him. He used it, coming out onto the platform and dropping down the steps.

The cry, "All aboard," ran down the line of

cars. He saw the conductor give his high-ball signal with his arm, and heard the hiss of steam and the grinding as the drivers hit the solidness of the rails. The train moved, but he was hardly conscious of it. He drew the folded note from his pocket and opened it, trying to decipher the scrawled lines.

"SAM SELLER KILLED CAP. I LET HIM IN THE HOUSE THROUGH THE REAR DOOR."

It was not signed. He turned with some vague idea of swinging back aboard the train, but as he turned the last coach passed him. He watched the train gather speed and disappear around the curve which marked the end of Railroad Avenue.

Chapter Eight

The crowd was already thinning. He felt their movement and was barely conscious of it as he stood there, gazing after the departed train.

His impulse was to rush into the telegraph office, to have the agent wire the next station to take Flora off the train, but caution came to his rescue. A message of that kind would be common property within the hour. The telegraph operator simply could not keep his mouth shut. Far better to wait until he heard from Mary. He could always trace Flora through her.

And there was another angle. Flora was angry with Sam Seller for not being at the station to see her off. The whole story could well be a fabrication, an effort to get even with Seller for apparently forsaking her.

A voice at his elbow startled him. He turned to look into Lloyd Warner's disapproving face.

"A moment, Marshal."

The formal address warned Joe. He saw Boyce beyond Warner and realized that the mayor was extremely unhappy.

"What is it?" he asked.

"That exhibition before the whole town will certainly do you no good."

"What exhibition?"

"Was it necessary for you to help that woman onto the train and—and treat her as if she were a lady?"

Condon fought down an urge to laugh. Lloyd Warner was so very pompous; he took himself with such great seriousness. But this was no time to antagonize the cattle buyer so he said with deceptive meekness, "You ordered me to send her out of town, remember."

Lloyd Warner's face reddened, but he managed to recover his control. "Your attitude is wrong, Marshal," he said quietly. "Don't make the same mistakes Cap made. Don't be too friendly with the wrong people."

Condon measured him, wondering again if Warner was worried because he had talked with Mary Hoolian. It seemed entirely fantastic, and yet it kept recurring to his mind. Lloyd Warner was in a perfect position to benefit by stealing cattle.

He said suddenly, "How long do you think this town will last?"

Both Warner and the mayor stared at him as if he had just taken leave of his senses. "Last?" Warner said.

"I've heard talk," Condon said, "that this will be the last season the trail herds will reach Dexter. Railroads are building to the south of us. I was talking to Pete Ortman shortly before he died. He told me the saloon men and gamblers were trying to open up the town because they figured this was their last year here."

Surprisingly the mayor said, "I've been trying to tell you, Lloyd."

Annoyance flashed across Warner's face. "Tell me what?"

Boyce looked unhappy, as if he hated to call attention to himself, but Condon listened. Somehow or other, when Boyce *did* stick his neck out, he always merited a respect which he seemed reluctant to accord himself. Boyce never quite succeeded in being the mouse he apparently thought he was.

"I said that this was our last year, Lloyd. I said that maybe the trouble was that Cap and some of the others figured the same thing and were trying to get theirs while the time was right."

Condon cut in. "Do you honestly believe Cap was in on that cattle theft?"

The mayor blinked at him in surprise. "Don't you?"

Condon said, "I do not," and watched Warner.

The cattle buyer's face tightened. "I thought it was pretty well established."

"By whom?"

"Well—the money in his pocket, for one thing."

"I brought fifty thousand dollars of your money from Kansas City," Joe Condon said. "If someone had killed me and the K.C. police found the box nearby, they might have said that I'd stolen the gold."

"That's absurd. Whose money would it be?"

Condon said, "Who first suggested that Cap was in on the rustling?" and looked straight at Warner.

"I didn't."

"Someone did. The idea didn't just grow out of the air."

Warner bristled. Condon saw that he was getting nowhere. He turned and walked quickly away while he still had the shreds of his temper. He thought, I'm not cut out for this job. I can't hold my tongue. I say the wrong things to the wrong people. He rounded the corner of the station and stopped.

She stood in the south doorway. He smiled at her. It seemed that he always smiled when he saw Lucy Warner. Her mere presence gave him a lift of spirits, and he knew that it would always be the same, every time they met. He said, "How long have you been here?"

"Since before the train came. I had a letter I wanted to go out."

"Then you saw my disgraceful performance."

Her eyes darkened. "I saw what my father thought of it. I saw him talking to you. I'm sorry for his action. I was rather proud of the way you ignored the crowd, of the way you helped put them on the train. I think it's absurd the way most people on our side of the tracks pretend that such places don't exist, and the men who undoubtedly visit her fail to recognize her in public."

He said, "You're being sorry for her. Don't be. Mary is what she is. I don't judge her, but I give her little sympathy. She knows who killed Cap and who murdered Pete Ortman, and she's afraid to tell me."

Lucy Warner frowned uncertainly at him. "Are you serious?"

"I was never more serious in my life."

She put out a hand to touch his arm. "What's going on in Dexter? The place is changed. I sense it, but I don't know exactly why."

He started to tell her, then stopped. What if his first instinctive guess were right? What if her father were involved? What if Lloyd Warner was the man who had arranged the rustling of the cattle, plotted Cap's death, and engineered Pete Ortman's murder?

He looked at her eyes, gray and wide-spaced and candid, and knew a moment's uncertainty of purpose. If he had proof of Lloyd Warner's guilt, would he be strong enough to bring the man to justice, or would he turn in his badge and ride away?

He said evasively, "Maybe it's because Cap is dead. The town will never be quite the same without him."

She sensed his lack of openness and interpreted

it as a rebuke. "I have things to do," she said, and walked away.

He wanted to stop her, but he made no move. He stood watching as she crossed the street, and then he heard the low laugh behind him. He turned and saw Kern Alder standing in the station doorway.

"Where were you?"

She came forward until only a few feet separated them. She was tall for a woman, but she still had to look up into his face. "I was in the station. I couldn't help overhearing what was said."

"I don't suppose you tried very hard."

"Save your sarcasm. I've known you much too long. Of course I didn't. You're very much in love with her, aren't you?"

"That's none of your business."

"Maybe yes, maybe not." She laughed. "You have no chance, you know. I've seen this Hartford Hull. He has education and experience and he's handsome."

Anger robbed him of speech.

"I might do you a favor if you were a little more friendly," Kern purred. "I might take him away from your Lucy and leave you a clear field."

"You're never happy unless you're messing up someone's life," he growled. "Keep away from Hull. He's already spoken for."

She tossed her head, thoroughly enjoying herself. She had always delighted in baiting him.

“Must be very terrible to be so much in love that you try to save your girl’s beau for her even though it ruins your own chances. Father always said you were too soft. You have to be hard to get along in this life.”

“Pat ought to know,” he said shortly. “He’s grabbed about everything in sight.”

She grinned at the thought. “And he’s liable to grab this town if he takes the mind. He’s only two days down the trail. A rider came in this morning. Rick’s bringing the second herd along three days behind him.”

He started, wondering what effect Pat Alder’s arrival might have on the town. “You’d better get word to him to watch for raiders. I’ve got enough trouble without having Box A cattle rustled.”

“He doesn’t need word,” Kern said. “That man Howe has joined him. I don’t know what Howe told him, but Pat sent word to you. Pat said to keep your town off his back or he’d take it apart, board by board.”

Still smiling, she sauntered away. In a sour mood, Joe Condon crossed the south wing of Railroad Avenue and moved along it toward the Western Belle. He expected to find it closed, but the doors were open and the place bustled with activity.

Two painters were on a scaffold, recoating the metal ceiling. He watched them for a moment, then spoke to the bearded swamper who was mopping the floor. "What are you doing?"

"Cleaning up."

"For who?"

"Talbert."

"Frenchy Talbert? What's he got to do with the Western Belle?"

"Ask him. He's in the office."

Frenchy Talbert sat behind Pete Ortman's desk and he was not alone. Condon knew the three men by sight, but Sam Seller was the only one he could name. His belly muscles tightened as he remembered Flora's note, still in his pocket.

Seller was small and dark and slightly feminine of feature. He smiled, and Talbert said heartily, "Morning, Marshal."

Joe did not return the greeting. He said, "Maybe you have a right to be here, but if so you must have bought the place from Ortman's ghost."

Frenchy Talbert's laugh was too loud. "I'm merely renting it. Dutch Hanna owns it, and Ortman was behind on his rent. Hanna took over the fixtures as payment."

Condon had known Talbert casually ever since he joined the marshal's office. The man had run a bar farther down the street, a cheap place which produced trouble from time to time.

"Hanna didn't wait long to find a new tenant," he said ironically.

Talbert's white teeth flashed in his narrow dark

face. "He was drinking in my place when the news came that Pete had been killed. Naturally we got to talking, so I took over."

Condon did not believe him. He remembered Ortman's feeling that Cap Lennox had been killed in an effort to ease Ortman out. He also coupled Flora's note with the fact that Sam Seller was here, apparently working for Talbert.

He considered what he knew about Dutch Hanna. The man was a speculator, a trader in town lots. It did not surprise him to learn that Hanna owned the building, but when he considered that the man might be the big shot, the power behind the rustlers and the forces which seemed to be trying to take over the town, he dismissed the idea.

Hanna had neither the brains nor the force to control men. It might be Talbert. Talbert was shrewd and dangerous. But even Talbert failed to fit one of Ortman's specifications. He did not live north of the tracks.

Talbert was watching him, still smiling. Talbert said, "I'm glad you came, Joe. If you hadn't I would have sent for you." He put enough arrogance into that statement to make Condon bristle. "I'm taking over south of the tracks," he added.

"Are you?" Condon said, and waited.

"Look," Talbert said. "You and I are men who understand things. You are hired to keep the peace, and if I help you, you can help me in return."

"How do you help me?"

"I get all the gamblers and the saloon men together. I lay down certain rules. They follow the rules or they leave town."

"Like the agreement Cap had with Pete Ortman?"

"That's right. It saves you trouble and all of us grief."

"And what do I do for you in return?"

Talbert's long narrow fingers drummed on the desk top. "The town's got to open up a little, Joe. We all know that this is the last big season. Next year Dexter will be just another railroad town. We've all seen how the other camps shrank as the track went west. We've got to get ours this season."

"No," Joe Condon said.

Talbert stared at him. Talbert did not seem to be angry. "You're new on the job," Talbert said tolerantly. "You've got to get it through your head that this town has two parts, and that our part pays as much taxes as the boys north of the tracks. If you want to keep wearing that badge, you'll be sensible."

"No," Condon said. "And let me give you a small piece of advice. I've seen trail crews hurrah a town. I'm here to prevent that. But I'm also here to see that no one gets robbed. I've seen boys who have eaten dust and mud and sweat for a thousand miles robbed by crooked gamblers, by thimble-rigs. I've seen them fed knock-out drops, and beaten up in alleys when they objected. There was none of that in Dexter last year when Cap was here, and there will be none of that now. Just remember that. I'll close the first saloon I catch running a crooked game."

He took his time staring back into Frenchy Talbert's hot, hostile eyes, and then he turned on his heel and left the room.

Chapter Nine

Sam Seller stood in the shade of the wooden awning before Grant Bailey's dry goods store, with his beaver hat cocked back on his dark head, his fingers hooked in the lower pockets of his multicolored vest, and a fat cigar burning richly between his lips.

He was, Condon thought, the picture of a man who was very pleased with the world and with the position he held in it. There was a certain arrogance in Seller's manner of which Condon had never before been conscious, and he observed Seller from down the block for several minutes before moving up to him.

"You're on the wrong side of the street, Sam."

For an instant, Sam Seller's inner arrogance showed. But he curbed it, saying mildly, "That doesn't apply to us, Marshal, and you know it."

In a sense Seller was correct. The prohibition against crossing Railroad Avenue applied only to the dance-hall girls and bartenders and house men who worked the saloon games. Sam Seller was a gambler, but until this time he had never worked for any of the saloons, preferring to stay on the customers' side of the table, pitting his skill and his money against the house. As such he was in the position of any man who chose to risk his money against a game, and for that reason Condon had been surprised to see him in Frenchy Talbert's office.

"Aren't you working for Talbert?"

Seller removed the cigar from his lips. He examined the long unbroken ash with pride before he flicked it daintily away. "He asked me, but I said no."

"Still, most of you stayed on the other side of the tracks as long as Pete Ortman lived."

Seller looked him over. "Haven't you heard? Ortman's dead. There's a new deal around here, Marshal. You'd better get wise to yourself."

Condon's hand moved so quickly that Seller hardly realized what had happened until Condon caught him by the lapel of his well-cut coat and jerked him forward, off balance and helpless.

"There is a new deal," Condon said with his nose an inch away from Seller's. "I'm the new deal, buster." He thrust Seller away, and Seller nearly fell as Condon released his grip. "Walk on down to the marshal's office. I want to talk to you."

Seller fumbled awkwardly, trying to straighten his coat. All the color had drained from his face, making the blue blackness of his beard more noticeable.

"March." Condon dropped his hand to his gun. "Either walk or I'll buffalo you and take you in feet first."

Sellers stared at him, obviously toying with the temptation to draw a gun. He wore none in sight, but Condon felt certain that he had a holdout concealed somewhere about his person.

"Don't try it, Sam. I'd enjoy shooting you this morning."

Seller ran the tip of his tongue about his lips. "Now look, my wife and kids are in the store, buying things."

Condon did not glance toward the store window. He knew better than to take his eyes off the man. He remembered the woman and the tired children he had seen on the train. He sympathized with them. But he also recalled Flora and the scribbled note in his pocket.

"Sorry," he said. "Get moving."

"You'll be sorry for this, Condon. You'll find out I've got friends."

"Get moving."

Seller glanced at the store again. Then he shrugged and walked down the street with Condon at his heels.

They passed a dozen people. One or two spoke to Seller. All nodded to Condon and turned to look curiously after the marshal. For his part, Condon never took his eyes from Seller's back. He followed him up the long block and through the door into the marshal's office.

Blankton sat at the desk. Across the room, a tall, thin, redheaded man with a narrow, freckled face was sitting in a chair tilted against the wall.

Condon recognized him. It was Harvey, Blankton's younger brother. He had forgotten until this moment that he had told Blankton to offer him a job.

Blankton got up, saying, "Harvey'll take the job. He—" and then stopped. Condon stepped up behind Seller, running his hands up under the man's coat, finding the small .41 caliber Remington derringer in the holster strapped to Seller's left wrist.

He jerked it free and tossed it to the desk. Seller took an angry step forward and Condon slapped him with the back of his right hand, hard, across the mouth.

The blow cut the gambler's lip, forcing it against his sharp white teeth. He spat blood on the floor.

"You wouldn't do that if I had a gun," he said.

Condon grabbed the front of his coat with his left hand and slapped him twice more. The second time he brought the edge of his hand down across the bridge of Seller's nose with force enough to start tears flowing.

"Why did you kill Cap Lennox?" he demanded.

Behind him Condon heard Blankton's sharp-drawn breath, but he was too occupied with Seller to pay any attention.

Seller's eyes were watering, his nose already puffing. He tried to hit Condon in the side, but his blow lacked authority. Condon thrust him away, so hard that the gambler stumbled backward and came up with jarring force against the side wall.

He leaned there uncertainly, as if the impact had stunned him. His lip bled and his eyes watered and his nose was beginning to leak a little, dropping down on his fancy vest. In all he was a sorry sight, but he got no sympathy from Joe Condon.

Condon used the back of his hand to wipe a dew of sweat from his brow, and glanced around. Harvey Blankton's rather slack mouth hung open in utter amazement. The older Blankton was staring at Condon as if he had never seen him before.

He started forward. He did not have any clear picture of what he meant to do. He only knew that this man cringing before him had shot Cap Lennox.

Blankton caught his arm. Blankton dragged him back by main force. "Wait a minute, Joe, get hold of yourself." Blankton sounded scared, as if he realized that Condon was not quite sane, and feared what Condon might do.

It wasn't that Blankton had any sympathy for the prisoner, or that the idea of a beating shocked him. His sadistic streak would have made him enjoy it. He just had the feeling that if Condon were not controlled now he might go entirely berserk. For the first time in their association Blankton was afraid of him.

Joe Condon stopped. He turned and saw Blankton. Then slowly his shoulders relaxed. His eyes lost their glassy expression and suddenly he seemed very, very tired.

"Throw him in the cell." He did not even look at the prisoner. He went around the desk and sank into the seat which Blankton had occupied.

Blankton took Seller's arm and started for the grilled door giving on the jail corridor. Seller pulled loose. He pushed past Blankton before the deputy could stop him and came up against the far side of the desk, leaning his fists upon it, bending toward the seated Condon.

"Have you gone crazy?"

Blankton and his brother held their breaths. Both of them fully expected Condon to explode, but all anger seemed to have been washed out of him. He acted as if he had been drained by the violence of his own emotions.

"Why?" he asked in a dead voice. "For saying you shot Cap?"

"I didn't shoot him," Seller said. "Why would I want to shoot him? How would I have gotten into that house without anyone seeing me?"

"One of the girls let you in through the rear door."

That statement surprised Seller, really shocked him, although he tried to brazen it out.

"That's the silliest thing I ever heard—"

"Lock him up," Condon said.

Blankton caught Seller's arm again. The gambler wrenched free, his strength increased by desperation. He whirled and tried to duck past Blankton, heading blindly for the door.

Harvey Blankton stuck out one foot and Seller sprawled over it. The Blankton brothers lifted him between them and jerked him upright. Now that Harvey Blankton had recovered from his astonishment he was grinning, a devil dancing in his green eyes.

"Active cuss, and awkward too." He started to shove the prisoner toward the cells, but Condon said, "Wait." He walked around in front of Seller.

"How much did you get for killing Pete Ortman?"

"I don't even know who killed Pete. I—"

"But you do know who killed Cap?"

"You're crazy. I didn't mean that. I meant—"

"Lock him up."

They pushed him through into the jail corridor and locked him in the end cell. When they came back they found Condon standing at the window, staring out at the street.

He turned around and studied Harvey Blankton in silence. He rather liked the redhead, from what little he knew of him. Harvey had been a freight handler, with a humor which took the form of practical jokes.

"Your brother tell you about the job?"

Harvey nodded.

"Want it?"

Again the nod.

Joe moved over to the desk, got a deputy's badge, the same one he had worn before Cap's death, and handed it to the redhead. "You furnish your own gun and pay for your own drinks. I don't want you taking anything from a saloon man. Not *anything,* understand."

No one spoke. Condon said, "Frenchy Talbert's taken over the Western Belle, and he's trying to take over Pete's spot."

He watched the older Blankton's face, but there was no change of expression.

"They want to open up the town. The first time you catch a crooked game, close the place."

Blankton stirred. "That will make trouble."

"I know it. Some trouble, that is." Condon paused. "But there are two trail herds a couple of days south of here. They belong to Pat Alder, one of the toughest Texans alive. If his crews get pushed around you'll have trouble here such as you never dreamed of."

Blankton grunted noncommitally. Condon drew Flora's note from his pocket and passed it to him. Blankton read it in silence, then gave it back. "Who gave it to you—Flora?"

Condon raised one eyebrow. "What made you think it was her?"

Blankton's shrug was expressive. "I've seen her with Seller. In fact I had to warn her off the street a couple of times. How come she crossed him? Because his wife showed up yesterday?"

Condon felt color rise up under his tan. He said slowly, "It's probably partly my fault." He told them about the note which Flora had given him on the preceding night, and how he had ground it into the mud with his boot. "I figured I was doing the right thing." He said it now as an apology.

"And you think Sellers killed Ortman too?"

"It figures." He went on to tell them about Frenchy Talbert moving into the Western Belle. "I found Seller in the office with Talbert. He doesn't work for Frenchy, at least not at the gambling tables, and this morning when I collared him he was all dressed up. His wife and kids were in the store, buying things, and he acted as if he had all the money in the world."

"I didn't search him," Blankton said.

"Do it. Harvey, give him a hand."

The redhead grinned. "Gladly. It's the first time I ever got a chance to lay my hands on any gambling money." He followed his brother into the corridor. Condon turned back toward the window. Through it he saw Hartford Hull come down Denver Street and step into the bank across the thorofare.

Blankton came back with a heavy wallet in his hand. He opened it on the desk and began to count it. The wallet contained more than four thousand dollars.

"That nearly cinches it," Condon said. "Seller has always been a small timer. If he'd won a lot of money in the last few days somebody would have heard of it."

Blankton nodded. "But four thousand—who paid him? Not Talbert. He hasn't got that kind of money either."

"He has now. He took over the Western Belle."

"I'll make Seller talk."

"Wait a minute." Condon stopped him. "There's a lot more to this, I think, than merely killing Cap and grabbing the Western Belle."

"I'll get it out of him." Blankton's face was wolfish with anticipation.

"Not yet. I doubt that he knows too much. A while ago I was ready to kill him." He sighed heavily. "For the first time in my life I took pleasure in thinking about killing a man. You stopped me, and I'm thanking you. I don't want him dead. I want to know what's going on in this town, who's behind it, and what they plan."

The two brothers watched him.

"I was going to leave," he said. "I'm not now. I'm going to stay. I'm going to fight. Somebody is getting ready to take over this town. He won't do it, because Dexter Springs belongs to me."

Blankton whistled between his teeth. "I never

heard you talk this way before. You sound like Cap."

Condon eked out a tired smile. He said, "There will be a fight, and people are going to get hurt. If you want out, the time to leave is now."

The brothers glanced at each other and then back at him. Blankton said, "Who do you think the boss is?"

"I don't know. Maybe Talbert. He seems to be taking over, but I doubt it. He isn't big enough. What would he do with stolen cattle? Anyhow, someone is going to try to free Seller. That's why I don't want you to try to make Sam talk now. I want to hold him as bait, to see who's interested in taking care of him."

Blankton looked doubtful. This projection was too indirect for him. If Seller had the information, the easiest way was to beat it out of him.

"If any visitors turn up," Condon said, "let Sam see them—and you try to hear what is said. I'm going to talk to Dutch Hanna. I'm going to find out how tough he is."

He settled his hat more firmly, hitched his gun rig into the most convenient position, and went outside.

Chapter Ten

Dutch Hanna was fat. He filled the chair beside his scarred desk in the little office he maintained beside the bank. Typical of the land speculators who had followed the railroad west, he had bought and sold lots in every town site along the line. He grinned when Condon came in, saying breezily,

"Have a chair, Marshal, take the law off your feet."

Condon leaned against a corner of the desk. "You're heading for trouble, Dutch."

Hanna's grin faded slowly as he realized that Condon was serious. "What are you talking about, Joe?"

"Talbert."

The fat man digested this in silence.

"When did you buy the building that houses the Western Belle?"

"Nearly a year ago. The record's in the courthouse."

"How much back rent did Ortman owe you? I thought he was well off."

The fat man spread his hands. "Five months' worth. The winter was tough as you well know. He kept promising to pay as soon as the herds started coming up."

Joe Condon could not prove it, but he had the distinct impression that the fat man was lying. Sweat showed on his high pink forehead and he shifted uneasily in the chair.

"What's the matter?" Hanna asked. "You seem—"

"Frenchy is making muscles," Condon said. "He's acting as if he wants to step into Ortman's shoes."

"Gee, Joe. You can't blame me for that. I just rented the place to him. I had to do something with Pete dead. I can't run the place myself." He laughed too loudly. "The space behind the bar isn't wide enough for me to get into."

Condon considered him. "I hope you're telling the truth, Dutch."

The fat man held up protesting hands. "Why should I lie to you?"

"That's what I'm trying to find out. Just be sure you don't, Dutch. Someone stole those cattle. Someone killed Cap and Pete Ortman. Whoever it is has got pretty big plans and if you got in his way you might get hurt."

He left it hanging there and walked out. He crossed the street and stood on the corner, a still figure in the sun, representing the authority of the town.

The fat man watched him through the window. He waited until Condon moved on, then left his office and walked to the corner to make sure that Condon had not doubled back along the side street to check his movements.

But he saw the tall figure of the marshal well down toward the corner of Second and Railroad Avenue. He retraced his steps. He was sweating heavily, creating wet patches on his shirt under his flabby arms.

He entered the newspaper office and walked to the counter.

"I've got a couple of lots I think I'll sell," he said to Hartford Hull in a voice loud enough to reach the printer at the rear. "What's a four-inch ad going to run me?"

Hull said, "In a minute." He called to the printer: "Run down to the corner, Jake, and get me some coffee." He waited until the printer vanished through the rear door, then said, "Well?"

The fat man mopped his head with his handkerchief. "Condon was in to see me, asking questions. I'm afraid he's getting wise."

Hartford Hull frowned slightly. He seldom showed more than a trace of his feelings.

"You made a mistake," Dutch Hanna said, "getting him appointed marshal. Talbert thinks so too."

"He does," Hull said, in a tone which the fat man had learned from past experience boded danger. "Talbert isn't supposed to think. I'll do the thinking for all of us."

Dutch Hanna was not a brave man, and he

knew that if Hull were pushed too far he was very dangerous. He said weakly, "Talbert thinks Blankton would be better."

"Oh, he does? Blankton has his hand out. He can be bought and a man who can be bought can't be trusted. The other side might offer him more money. No, Condon is the best choice—an ignorant cowboy off the trail. Stop worrying, Dutch. We have everything under control."

"He's suspicious," Hanna said fretfully. "Frenchy moved too fast. It's all right for you. He isn't even looking in your direction. But he's staring directly at me, and his eyes are plenty hard."

Hull considered him and wondered anew at the weakness of the men with whom he had surrounded himself. Hull came of a good Mid-western family. His education was far superior to the average of the day. He had joined the Union Army and done very well, rising through the ranks until he attained a major's commission. Very early, in the Army, he developed an eye for a quick profit, and Frenchy Talbert had given him the chance.

Frenchy Talbert had been raised in the gutters of New York, the Five Points section which spawned thieves and bully boys and politicians, and Frenchy had practiced politics until chance turned him into an Army sutler. He had become attached to Hull's regiment and they had drifted into an unofficial partnership.

There had been small deals in whiskey for the troops, and later deals in captured Southern cotton. Twice they had been nearly caught, but at the end of the war they counted a neat profit and began looking around for a new field of operation. The Kansas frontier with its budding railroad towns seemed the best bet. But they guessed wrong.

They decided that Dexter Springs would last; that unlike the other railhead towns it would not fade within a few years.

Hull established a newspaper, Talbert a saloon, and they sat down to wait, taking in other men as they needed them. Outwardly they were the most casual of acquaintances, barely speaking when they met. Frenchy set himself to become a power south of the tracks while Hull identified himself with the merchants, went to church and managed to get himself engaged to Warner's daughter.

But from the first Frenchy found himself blocked by Lennox and Ortman. Do what he would, he could not knock down their influence. And then it became obvious that Dexter Springs would not last, that it would soon be outflanked by other shipping points, closer to Texas and the herds of wild cattle which had multiplied during the war.

They revised their plans. They must make

their killing in the coming season or not make it at all. And then Talbert conceived the idea of establishing a ranch farther north, in Nebraska, which was just opening up.

They would raid each trail herd as it neared Dexter Springs, stampeding the cattle and running off a small portion of them, hurrying their stolen animals northward with a heavy crew which could push the animals to safety and then split, some of them returning to town to wait for a second raid while the others drove on to the new ranch.

But this was not enough. They also meant to levy their toll on the trail herd crews which reached Dexter Springs that season. To do this they had to get rid of both Cap Lennox and Pete Ortman. Cap's death had not been difficult to arrange. They waited until Condon went to Kansas City for more gold to meet the demands of Warner's cattle buying. Then they sent word to Lennox that a man hiding at Mary Hoolian's knew who had stolen the cattle from the trail herd and would talk.

It had been simple for Sam Seller to slip into the house and shoot the marshal in the back; simple for Hull to accompany Warner when the news of the murder came, to search the body and ask why a marshal should have so much money in his pocket.

In spite of himself Hull grinned at the memory.

In some ways Lloyd Warner was very smart. In others he was as gullible as a newborn baby. It had taken only a few, careful suggestions on Hull's part to make Warner believe he was the first one to suspect that Cap Lennox was dishonest. From then on Hull had defended the marshal, but in a way that only made Warner and the other members of the council more certain of Lennox's guilt.

Now, Hull thought, if he could handle Lucy and her father and the mayor, and the rest of the people north of the tracks, he certainly had nothing to fear from Joe Condon.

He said so brusquely to the fat man. He had no respect for Dutch Hanna. They had picked Dutch up when they first arrived in Dexter, and used him as a front man for their real estate operations, letting him buy property in his name and then taking undated quit-claim deeds which they could register at any time.

"Condon couldn't find his own shadow," Hull assured Hanna.

"Then you haven't heard? He arrested Sam Seller better than two hours ago."

Hartford Hull stared at him. "Where did you get that?"

"Grant Bailey told me. He saw Condon pick Seller up."

Hartford Hull mulled the information over slowly, trying to see what it would mean to him.

As far as he knew, Sam Seller was not aware of Hull's connection with the organization. The small-time gambler had worked for Talbert off and on. Talbert had hired Seller originally because of his association with one of Mary's girls.

"What evidence has Condon got against Seller?"

The fat man did not know.

"I'll find out," Hull said. "Stop worrying about it. And don't come here again unless you have to."

He watched Dutch Hanna leave. He had no intention of asking Condon directly. He would find out through Lloyd Warner. A word to Warner, and the cattle buyer would be at the jail, asking the marshal questions. Warner did not like to think that anything went forward at the Springs without his say so. That was something which Condon would have to learn.

Hartford Hull waited for the printer's return. He was a careful man. He never aroused people's suspicions if he could avoid it. He drank the unwanted coffee and then he started for the bank.

But halfway there he changed his mind. He turned into the side street which led him to Railroad Avenue two blocks way. He and Talbert had not been careless in their meetings. They saw each other only as much as necessary, so he felt no fear in going to the Western Belle. After all, he was a newspaper man, and the change in ownership of the largest saloon in town was a legitimate story.

He came through the doors and looked around. The painters had finished the ceiling and gone, but the odor of their handiwork lingered, mingling with the odor of sawdust and the smell of stale beer.

Already the clientele had changed. Under Ortman, the Western Belle had drawn most of its patrons from the substantial citizens of the town, men from north of the tracks.

Several merchants were present, but he also recognized a number of cheap gamblers and several of the riders Talbert had employed for the cattle raid.

He frowned. If this continued, the Western Belle would be no better than the saloon which Frenchy had formerly operated. He hooked his elbows on the bar, nodding to several men, buying a drink all around. "Quite a change," he said.

He heard the murmured comments, and gauged their feelings and found that they were not happy with the move. "Well, I'd better get the story," he said lightly. "One thing about a newspaper man—he never stops working."

They nodded and he said to the bartender, who did not know him, "Talbert in?"

The man hesitated, then indicated the office door. Hull went to it, knocking, calling loud enough for them all to hear: "From the *Sentinel*. The last chance you'll have at free advertising."

"Come in."

He pushed the door open and entered. As soon as it closed his manner changed, becoming very business-like. "Did you hear that Condon arrested Seller?"

Talbert swore. "What for?"

"Lennox's death. Will Seller talk?"

"Not as long as he thinks we're stronger than Condon. But if he once gets the idea that we can't help him—" Talbert shook his head. "Maybe it would be simpler to shoot him through the jail window."

"No," Hull said. "That would really stir up the town, and we want no more trouble than we can help right now. If Lennox hadn't seen Charley Byers drunk and spending more money than he'd ever had before, none of this would have happened."

Talbert objected to that. "You're wrong, Major. We had to get rid of Cap Lennox, and Pete Ortman too. We made the mistake of not killing them at the same time and making it look like they'd gunned each other."

"No one would have believed that. They were too close."

"And you made a mistake having Condon appointed marshal. Blankton would have been better."

Hull flushed. He was a vain man and he could not stand much criticism, even from as close an associate as Frenchy Talbert.

"I didn't have much choice," he said sharply. "It was either Condon or Blankton, and Blankton is dangerous. Maybe he can be bought, but he wouldn't stay bought. And the man is a natural killer. If it came to a fight he might raise hell with everything. No, Condon is better for our purpose. He's honest, and an honest man is always easier to handle than a crook. He isn't as suspicious."

"Well, he was in here, and he laid down the law and he meant it. He said he'd close the first saloon he found running a crooked game."

"Let him find one. Let him find half a dozen."

Talbert gaped at him. "Have you gone crazy?"

"But don't let him find one in here." Hull was smiling now, completely recovered from his annoyance.

Talbert thought it over. Slowly his dark, narrow face broke into a smile.

"You're a bastard," he said admiringly.

Hull laughed, pleased, taking it as a compliment. "We don't care what happens to this town, do we? We want to get enough this season to establish the biggest ranch this country has ever seen."

The saloon keeper nodded.

"So the more places Condon puts out of business the more trade comes into the Western

Belle. Ortman was a damn fool. He policed his competitors. He made them behave and they stayed in business to take customers away from him."

"What you're doing is murdering the town."

"It's dead anyhow. And we won't get the blame. Condon will, and no one will like him for it."

"He'll probably get shot."

"Would you care?"

"I'd dance on his grave," Frenchy Talbert said with real feeling.

"All right." Hull never enjoyed himself as much as when he was planning trouble for others. "We'll keep Joe Condon so busy in the next few days that he'll have no time to worry us. First, hire one of the dealers in each of the larger saloons. Tell them exactly what you want them to do. They're to wait until one of the deputies comes in and then gaff a game. Make it so obvious that the deputy won't miss the play."

"Some of them won't like it," Talbert said. "Some of them might be tempted to talk."

Hull's face hardened. "Just remind them of Ortman's death. Ortman was a kind of god to everyone south of the tracks. It scared them when he died. If he can be gunned down, not one of them is safe and they know it."

Talbert eyed him curiously. "Did you kill Pete yourself?"

Hull reached across the desk and grabbed

Talbert's wrist, pulling the lighter man to his feet. "Don't ever say that again," he warned. "Don't even think it." He shoved Talbert back into the desk chair, hard.

"That's the first step, Frenchy. Get working on it this afternoon. Second, there are two large herds south of town. They both belong to the man Condon use to work for. In fact I think that once Condon meant to marry the daughter. She's in town and from what I hear she's something of a man chaser."

Talbert said nothing. He was nursing his twisted wrist.

"Those herds will be coming in shortly. Warner has already sent some men out to meet them, to help. He doesn't want a recurrence of our last raid."

Talbert said, "That isn't good."

"It's fine," Hull said. "We're going to make our big strike three ways. First, we're going to let the herds come in and be sold to Warner. This Pat Alder will pay off his crews and we'll drain them, right here in the Western Belle. Next, Alder will take most of his payment in gold. That's what the money Condon brought from Kansas City was for."

"How did you know all this?"

Hull gave him a self-satisfied smile. "Warner tells me things. Warner considers that I'm already married to his daughter. Pat Alder has been writing to him, wanting payment in gold. Alder has arranged to take up some leases in the Nations and the Indians demand gold."

Talbert did not change expression. "So?"

"So when they start back down the trail, we send men after them. They left Dexter. The fact that they fail to reach Red River Crossing is none of our business."

"Neat. Then we don't touch the cattle."

Hull snorted. "Who said we don't touch the cattle? I'd rather have Lloyd Warner after us than those Texas cowhands. Certainly we take the cattle, all of them, from the stock pens, before Warner can ship them east."

Chapter Eleven

Hartford Hull crossed the street and walked into the marshal's office. He found Joe Condon alone at the desk.

"I've got two messages, from Lloyd Warner," he said in an offhand way. "Don't blame me for either of them."

"Why should I blame you?" Condon asked.

Hull shrugged. He took a chair, leaning it against the wall so he could see into the jail corridor. "But first, my own business. Why didn't you tell me you meant to arrest that gambler? It's news, and I'm in the newspaper business."

"You mean Seller?"

"I guess so. Lloyd Warner said you were holding some gambler for Cap Lennox's murder."

"That's right."

"Got any real evidence?"

"A note from one of Mary Hoolian's girls."

Hull had not expected that. It came as something of a shock, but his face remained impassive. "Enough to convict him?"

"That's up to the county attorney. He'll be here next week."

"And you're going to hold him until then?"

"What do you want me to do—turn him loose?"

Hull laughed. "You can be a surly bastard, Joe.

I don't care what you do. I just don't want to see you in trouble."

"And just why should arresting a murderer get me into trouble?"

Hull leaned forward, suddenly serious. "I don't know why, and don't tell him I told you—but Lloyd Warner wants him out."

For a full minute Joe Condon sat very quiet, not a muscle moving, while inwardly all his suspicions of Lloyd Warner leaped into active life. Then he said slowly, "Why are you telling me this?"

Hull measured him, as he tried to measure every man he met. Life to him was a gigantic poker game and everyone in it was an opponent. Frenchy Talbert was his partner, because he needed someone he could trust to deal with the gamblers and with the riders they used to raid the herds. But he would sacrifice Talbert in a moment if it would further his plans. He used men like Dutch Hanna, fully meaning to cast them aside later. And he meant to use Joe Condon. But he knew that with Condon he would need a different approach.

His voice had a trace of embarrassment, put there purposely. "What I'm going to tell you I wouldn't say to anyone else in Dexter. A newspaper man interests himself in other people. He has to. His job is to find out things and print them. But a man is human, even if he does publish a paper, and there are certain things I would hesitate a time before setting up in type."

Condon said, "What things?" and felt the muscles across his shoulders tightening like bowstrings.

Hull took his time. Inwardly he was enjoying himself. Outwardly he seemed distressed. "I'm going to marry Lucy Warner." He said it defensively. "No matter what her father has done it doesn't affect my feeling for her."

"What's he done?"

"The trouble is," Hull said, "I can't actually prove he's done anything. I have no evidence, and a man should be extremely careful in voicing suspicions."

"What's he done?" Condon let annoyance creep into his voice. This was what Hull wanted: to have it appear that the marshal had forced information from him, information which he was reluctant to pass on.

"First," he said, "let's consider several things. Cap Lennox was murdered. Warner and I went to examine the body. It wasn't Warner's business, but he insisted on being there. He was the one who found the money in Cap's pocket, and then hinted that the sum was too large for Cap to come by honestly."

He paused. "Go on," Condon said.

"Second, Pete Ortman is killed and Frenchy Talbert moves into the Western Belle, which is owned by Dutch Hanna. But I happen to know that for nearly a year now Warner has been backing Hanna in his real estate operations, and that he holds mortgages on a number of Hanna's properties."

He did not add that he had been the one who first suggested to Warner that it would be a good investment.

"Go on, man."

"I hear rumors." Hull seemed more reluctant than ever. "Warner had the backing of two packing companies in his cattle buying, and he operates through the Kansas City banks. This town is nearly through. We all know it, and Warner is heavily involved in local property. What would you do if you found yourself in his spot?"

"I'm not in his spot," Joe Condon said.

"Of course you're not. But if you were, wouldn't it be wise to do three things? First, get all the money in cash that you can from your banks, preferably in gold?"

He saw the flicker of Condon's eyes.

"Second, get rid of Cap Lennox and Pete Ortman, move your men into the Western Belle, open up the town and milk the trail crews for all their pay?"

Condon didn't move.

"And lastly, steal your own cattle, after they'd been paid for, and drive them north to a ranch you'd established under another name. Sure, you'd go bankrupt and your creditors would close in—but what would they get? Nothing but the real estate you hold in a dying town, real estate which won't be worth the mortgages three years from now."

Condon squinted at the ceiling. "I don't believe it," he said finally.

"Neither do I." Hull agreed quickly, too quickly. "But I had to pass it along to you." He stood up. "One more thing. I almost forgot. Warner has invited that Texas girl to dinner. He's had letters from her father. He'd like you to pick her up at the hotel at a quarter to six."

With that Hartford Hull departed.

But for a long while afterward, Joe Condon sat brooding in his chair. Hull had not said one thing about Warner that could not be checked: the real estate he held; the fact that he had backed Dutch Hanna and was in a position to put pressure on the speculator; the fact that Warner had seemed too ready to accept the slender evidence of Cap Lennox's guilt. And yet, it seemed impossible that Lucy Warner's father would stoop to such things.

All during dinner Condon watched Lloyd Warner without appearing to. It was, for him, a far from pleasant meal.

Kern Alder was at her sparkling best, drawing laughter with her sallies, telling them with engaging frankness how jealous Condon had always been where she was concerned.

They all laughed at him, and he knew that he was flushing under his heavy tan. He caught Lucy's eyes upon him, noting the amusement in their depths, and he became deeply angry with the girl at his side.

But he forced himself to ignore her teasing. He centered his attention on Lloyd Warner, listening as the man talked about the town. Warner's coldly calculating manner had always repelled him. Warner talked in terms of profit and he spoke of the Springs as if the town were nearly a private enterprise.

After they left the table Warner motioned Joe into a corner. "I understand you made an arrest this morning?" he said in a low voice.

Condon nodded, poker-faced.

"Shouldn't you have talked it over with the mayor and me?"

The marshal, drew a long breath. All his discontentment with the evening welled up through him.

He said carefully, "Seller is guilty as hell, but I'm not interested in the fact that he fired the actual shot. I want the man or men behind him. I want the ones who planned that cattle raid and who are threatening to open up the town."

It was a direct challenge. He saw Warner's eyes harden, but he could not be certain whether this meant the man was guilty or simply that Warner could not stand anyone questioning his authority.

"I'd like to see the evidence," Warner said.

"I'll show it to the county attorney when he arrives. If he thinks you or anyone else has the right to see it, I'll go by his judgment."

Warner said harshly, "We'll see, we'll see," and turned away.

Later, as Condon and Kern Alder walked along the dark street toward the hotel, Kern said, "You aren't very popular with Mr. God, are you?"

He almost gave way to irritation, but on second thought he decided that Kern might be useful now.

"You're always good at sizing up men, Kern. What do you think of him?"

"Why, I think he always has to have his own way. He can't play in any game unless he deals the cards."

"Would you guess that he could be dishonest?"

She laughed. "That depends on what you call dishonesty. I think he'd go a long way to put over a business deal."

"Far enough to steal cattle?"

She stopped and he had to stop too. She stood there, looking up at him in the darkness. "What are you trying to tell me, Joe?"

"Nothing. I'm just asking your opinion."

She said, "You're a goose. You're driving yourself crazy. You love that girl. I saw the way you looked to see how she was taking my jokes tonight—and now you're trying to make her father into a thief."

"I'm not making him anything. Your father is down the trail with ten thousand head of cattle, and I want to know what goes on here before he arrives."

"You'd better hurry," she said. "He's riding in in the morning. Mr. Warner heard from him tonight."

Condon swore under his breath.

She put a hand on his arm. "You take life too seriously, Joe. Why don't you turn in that silly badge and take over one of the leases Dad has in the Nations?"

"Still trying to get me back?" he asked sourly.

She chuckled. She stood on tiptoe, locked her hands behind his neck, pulled his face down and pressed her lips full against his. Her mouth was slightly open. Her body was warm and pliant, yet filled with surging life as it leaned tightly into the curve of his own.

He kissed her in return. The action was almost spasmodic, and she let go her hold, pushing him away.

"I can get you back any time I want you," she said. "The trouble is, I'm not sure I want to. That Hartford Hull can be an awfully attractive man."

Chapter Twelve

Sam Seller was unhappy. He sat in the cell brooding as the light in the street outside faded into darkness. He hated Condon for putting him there, but his resentment against Frenchy Talbert was growing too. He did not know everything about Talbert's operations, but he thought he knew enough to cause the saloon man considerable trouble. He could name the men who had raided the trail herd, and he could testify that Dutch Hanna had spent most of the night after Ortman's death in Talbert's office.

He had been well paid for setting up Cap Lennox's murder, and his natural arrogance had led him to believe that Frenchy would turn the town upside down to free him. Yet he had been in jail most of the day and Frenchy had made no move to release him.

The thought of trying to make a deal with Condon occurred to him, but he dismissed it. He feared Joe Condon as he had feared no one else in his checkered life.

But he had to do something; he had a deep and abiding fear of death. Maybe if he talked to the mayor . . . And then he thought of Lloyd Warner.

The more he thought about Warner the more it seemed to him that the cattle buyer was the one man to try to bargain with. Warner had a heavy stake in the town. Warner had to deal with the men bringing the herds up the trail. Warner had been no friend of Cap Lennox. He might well be willing to trade Seller's freedom for the information Seller could give him about the cattle thieves.

Phil Moore was alone in the marshal's office. Both Blankton brothers had gone out somewhere.

"Come here a minute," Seller called.

Phil Moore was in no hurry to answer. He sat with his feet on the desk, a cheap cigar burning in the corner of his thin-lipped mouth, imagining that he was the marshal of Dexter, taking orders from no one.

"Hey, come here a minute!"

Reluctantly Phil Moore pulled his feet down from the desk. He rose, muttering as he came along the jail corridor.

"This better be good, Seller."

"I want to talk to Lloyd Warner," Seller said.

Phil Moore took the stogie out of his mouth and got set to swear.

"Did you hear what I said? I want to talk to Warner! If you know what's good for you you'll get the message to him!"

Such self-confidence impressed Phil Moore in spite of himself. "I'd better talk to Condon," he said.

"Never mind Condon. He isn't as important as

he thinks he is. Just tell Warner I want to talk to him. You won't be sorry."

Phil Moore knew something that Sam Seller did not know. Joe Condon was having dinner at Warner's house. He said, "All right, I'll tell him." He was not supposed to leave the marshal's office except in emergencies, but he considered this to be an emergency. It took him only a few minutes to walk the three blocks to Warner's house, but he arrived fifteen minutes after Joe Condon had gone.

He stood on the porch, explaining his mission to Warner, fumbling a little with his words, saying again and again that he would not have come if he had not believed Condon was there.

He knew vaguely that Hartford Hull was in the hallway behind Warner, but he paid no attention. The fact that Joe Condon was not here had disordered his thinking. He heard Warner say, "I'll go back with you," and heard Hull murmur something about seeing Condon first.

Warner's voice rose high pitched and intolerant. "Joe Condon doesn't run this town yet. I'll get my hat."

He vanished along the dark hallway and Hull said in an undertone to Lucy, "I'll walk downtown with your father."

"Do that." She did not sound too pleased. "At times Father takes on things which are hardly his affair."

Standing on the moonlit porch, she watched them go, and tried to resist a feeling of unease. She was a calm girl, carefully schooled in thought and actions, and she wondered at the restlessness which had bothered her of late.

Perhaps it was Cap Lennox's death and the fact that Joe Condon had succeeded him as marshal. He had interested her from the first, this Texas cowboy whose wild streak had been tamed by Lennox's understanding.

Joe Condon represented a life which was a little foreign, a little removed from her everyday existence. Despite the fact that she lived in a frontier town she knew almost nothing of what happened outside of her own small circle of acquaintances.

Her father had seen to that, and her engagement to Hartford Hull had made no difference. Hull lived in Dexter, but his whole point of view had been framed by his early life. He believed, and he made it increasingly plain as time went by, that a woman's place was in the home, and that a man shared neither his business worries nor his plans with a wife.

This was exactly the life her mother had lived with her father, and it lacked something which Lucy needed. She had listened attentively to the Texas girl that night, hearing the wild stories of the brush country in the sorry years just after the war, hearing of the wild rides to dances forty miles away, and suddenly she had known with clarity that this was what she wanted, what she had desired all her life—a chance to share with the man she chose, to ride with him and fight with him and love with him.

In her new-found awareness she had studied Hull and found him wanting. On the surface he was the perfect husband; handsome, interesting, probably a financial success. But she realized now, as she stood on the dark porch, that she had drifted into the relationship almost unwittingly. The choice had been her father's far more than hers.

She went back into the house, her mind on Joe Condon rather than on the man she was supposed to marry.

And for his part, Hartford Hull had never given Lucy a second thought since leaving the house. He was truly worried, and his mind darted this way and then that, like a mouse seeking some escape from a trap.

He guessed that Sam Seller had finally broken, that the fear had cracked through his nerves and he was ready to talk. The fact that the gambler had sent for Warner surprised him, and yet, as he walked along the block beside the cattle buyer he found a certain amount of satisfaction in the arrangement. It had been a lucky thing that Condon was not present when Phil Moore arrived. He had to make certain that Sam Seller did not talk, and there was only one sure way of sealing the man's lips.

He would have to do the job himself. He had always tried to avoid personal violence. Not that it bothered him, but it heightened the risks he took, and he seldom took a personal risk where he could hire others to do it for him.

In the case of Ortman he had had no choice. There had been no time to arrange the man's death, and it seemed that there was not enough time now.

He could not afford to have Seller talk to Warner. That was certain. Yet he had to clear himself and in a sense establish an alibi.

Phil Moore was ahead of them. Hull raised his voice to make sure the deputy marshal overheard. "I'd better get back to the office, Lloyd. We go to press first thing in the morning and there are several things I have to take care of tonight."

Warner murmured something, his mind on other things.

"You'll stop by the office after you see Seller and tell me what he has to say?"

"I doubt if it's important," Warner told him gruffly. "If Condon hadn't acted so mysterious about the arrest I wouldn't even be coming down here."

Hull said, "Of course," and made the right angle turn which would take him to the newspaper office. He traveled half a block, checked to see that Warner and Phil Moore were out of sight, then cut right into the alley.

He ran down its dark depths, reached Denver Street, looked both ways to make sure there was no one on the sidewalk to observe him, then ducked across its dust ribbon and into the alley which paralleled the jail. That afternoon he had noted that Seller was in the end cell. Now he headed directly for the proper barred window.

He reached it and paused for a moment, steadying his breath. The window was level with the top of his head. He looked around for something to stand on, but found nothing in the darkness.

He drew his gun, holding it in his right hand. He grasped one of the bars with his left hand, lifting himself the few inches necessary to peer into the cell beyond.

Seller was at the grilled door. Seller was saying, "I thought you'd come," and Hull caught the oily satisfaction in his tone. "I want to make a trade, Mr. Warner. Get me out of here and I'll tell you who raided that herd. I'll give you the names of the men who made the actual attack."

Hartford Hull raised his gun, knowing this would be the most difficult shot he had ever made. His feet were braced against the plank walls of the building, and he supported himself with his left hand while he steadied the heavy barrel of his forty-four across the sill of the jail window. He held his breath and squeezed the trigger.

The bullet missed Seller. It traveled between the bars of the cell door and knocked Warner's left leg out from under him, tearing through the fleshy part of the thigh.

Sam Seller swung about like a cornered animal. His instinct for survival made him throw himself sidewise, which put his head in direct line for Hull's second bullet. The slug struck him in the bridge of the nose. The shocking power of the heavy piece of lead knocked him backward against the bars. He was dead before he hit the floor.

Lloyd Warner lay writhing in the jail corridor. Phil Moore stood in the middle of the marshal's office, paralyzed by the suddenness of the shots. It did not occur to him to rush outside and catch the marksman as he fled from the alley. He ran into the corridor, horrified to find Lloyd Warner on the floor.

Hull dropped back into the alley after holding himself at the window long enough to make certain that his second bullet had killed Sam Seller.

He was perfectly cool. He knew that if Moore dashed from the building he could reach the alley's mouth in time to cut him off. For that reason he did not hurry, but with the gun still held ready in his hand he came along the alley's dark length toward the street, pausing again to assure himself that no one saw him, that no one blocked his path. Then, holstering his gun, he stepped boldly across Denver and came into the print shop at the rear.

The printer was at the window peering out. Hull said, "Those shots. Where did they come from?"

"I don't know. Sounded like they might be down at the corner."

Hull walked the length of the room. He stepped out onto the street with the printer at his elbow. He was in time to see Joe Condon charge around the corner and race into the marshal's office.

"Looks like trouble," Hull said easily. "I'd better find out. Leave a hole in the front page until we're sure."

The printer turned and went back reluctantly into the newspaper office. Hull took his time going down the street. He arrived to find that Condon and Phil Moore had helped Warner into a chair. Condon was trying to bandage the cattle buyer's leg while the deputy was just starting out after a doctor.

Hull stared at the wounded man and then at the kneeling marshal.

"What happened?"

"Maybe you had better ask Mr. Warner," Condon said.

Warner was in a great deal of pain, and the wound had shocked him as much as it had given physical hurt. But even in his present state of mind he did not miss Condon's implication.

"What do you mean by that, Marshal?"

Condon gave Hull a long, questioning look across Warner's head. "Maybe I don't mean anything." His voice was toneless. "But I think I'm entitled to an explanation. I arrest a man for Cap's murder and then he's shot in his cell."

"You don't think I shot him?" Warner said, angrily. "You don't think I shot myself in the leg?"

"I'm trying not to think anything, Mr. Warner, but it is strange that he should have sent for you. If he wanted to talk, why didn't he talk to me, or to the mayor?"

Warner opened his mouth. Warner was about to remind Condon that he was Dexter Spring's most important citizen, but then he stopped. For almost the first time in his career, caution touched Lloyd Warner. The pain, combined with the disturbing knowledge that this wound proved him to be as vulnerable as other men, drastically reduced his sense of self-importance—for the moment.

"I don't know why he should have asked for me," he said mildly, "but he did. Ask your deputy. He came to get me. Ask Hartford. He was still at the house when Moore came. He walked down to the corner with us."

"That's right," Hull said. "The deputy said Seller wanted to talk to Warner."

Phil Moore had been lingering beside the door, not certain whether he should stay or hurry for a doctor.

"Seller insisted on talking to Warner," Moore said defensively. "I wouldn't have listened to him, except I thought you were having dinner at the Warner house. I wouldn't have gone there if I'd known you'd already left."

"What did Seller say?"

"What difference does it make?" Warner cut in. "I'm bleeding like a stuck pig. How about getting a doctor?"

Condon ignored him. "What did Seller say?"

Moore fidgeted uncomfortably. "He said I had to get Warner. He said I'd be in bad trouble if I didn't."

Condon looked at Warner. "What was Sam Seller to you?" he asked, and Warner's temper overcame his newfound humility.

"Damn it, he was nothing. I barely knew who he was."

"Then why did you think it necessary to come rushing down here?"

"Marshal—*will* you get me a doctor?"

"I'll get him," Hartford Hull said.

He laughed softly to himself as he went out into the darkness. Things were working out even better than he had dared to hope.

Chapter Thirteen

Pat Alder was a big man and he rode a big horse. He rode into Dexter Springs as if he owned the town, and could prove it, but didn't intend to bother.

He did not come alone. He brought three riders with him, and one was Howe, the foreman of the trail herd which had been raided. He pulled up at the rack in front of the hotel and found his daughter waiting for him. He swung down and climbed the three porch steps and swept her into his arms with as much grace as a grizzly embracing a cub.

His red hair, now thoroughly shot with gray, sprouted wild and shaggy about his ears after the long weeks on the trail. His bristling red beard and his fierce blue eyes challenged the world.

Kern Alder was very glad to see her father. They were much alike. It was one of the deep sorrows of Pat Alder's life that she had not been a boy, a stalwart son to share his growing power, but Kern understood and forgave him.

She freed herself and stood laughing up at him. "Now Kansas is a place to be, when Pat Alder is here!"

Howe swung down from his horse. The other

riders remained in the saddle, grinning as Kern passed her father and came down the steps to greet them.

She had always been popular with the crew. Even as a very small girl she had known how to please men, and she was never so happy as when surrounded by an admiring crowd.

"Hello, boys. I'll bet you're dry."

They bobbed their heads shyly. In her presence they found few words. She turned back to her father.

"How was the trip?"

His big shoulders moved. "No real trouble. We cut out the she stock and calves and threw them onto the upper lease. Where's this man Warner and the gold he promised?"

She said, "Warner's laid up with a bullet in his leg. Joe Condon brought the gold from Kansas City on the same train that I came on."

He brightened. He had always liked Joe Condon. At one time he had hoped that Joe would be his son-in-law. "I hear Joe's turned into a ring-tail hot shot with a tin badge." He glanced at Howe and laughed.

The other cattleman flushed under his windburn tan. This was not what he had expected when he rode down the trail, looking for help from the Texas crews. He said sourly, "He's a little big for his britches."

Pat Alder winked at his two men. "We'll cut

him down to size, won't we, Phil? We raised him from a pup."

The taller man nodded. Alf Hudson grinned. "I'd sure admire to see Joe wearing a badge. I remember when he took that there Dallas sheriff and turned him inside out."

Pat had no interest in things well past. "You and Joe made it up?" he asked his daughter.

She flushed. "He's got another girl." She said it lightly, but her father caught the undertone of hurt. He understood her so well.

Of course she didn't cotton to giving up something she'd once had, even if she didn't really want it any more. And as for Joe Condon, he might wear a badge, and he might be marshal of one of the toughest towns in the state, but to Pat Alder that burr-headed boy was still just a Box A rider.

"Who's the girl?" he rumbled.

"Warner's daughter."

"You can beat her. I never saw a woman yet you couldn't take into camp—or a man for that matter. Rick's coming up the trail. He's bigger than Joe, and he still loves you." His laugh rolled out so that people halfway down the block turned to look. He was feeling fine. He always felt fine. Nothing could stand in his way.

"Let's go see this Warner," he said.

She said in a low tone, "I want to talk to you, Pat. There's trouble in this place. The marshal before Joe got killed, and Joe arrested some fellow for his murder. Then last night someone shot Warner and killed the prisoner. Whoever did it fired through the jail window—"

He patted her shoulder with a big hand. "Don't worry about it, honey. What these fool town people do is none of our business."

"It is our business," she said sharply. "Someone raided Howe's herd. The same people are liable to jump you."

"I've been trying to tell him," Howe said.

"Nobody raids the Box A," Pat Alder said contentedly. "I've got twenty men with the first herd and Rick has eleven more. Anybody starts trouble, we'll have a rustler hanging from every limb. Now, where is this Warner?"

"At home, in bed."

"I'll go see him."

But he saw Joe Condon first. They met on the street a block from Warner's house. Pat Alder let out the yell which once had scared half the Yankees at Vicksburg and came forward to shake Condon's hand. Then he caught Joe under the arms and swung him clear of the ground.

"Declare to goodness," he bellowed. "You're getting to be a real big boy."

Joe Condon laughed. He had always honored Pat Alder. As a boy he had served under him in the Texas Brigade, and he had worked for him steadily until he came to Dexter.

"Pat, you old cow thief! When did you ride in?"

"Few minutes ago. I'm looking for a cattle buyer named Warner. Know where he lives?"

"Just came from there."

"Show me." Alder swung him around and linked his big arm with Condon's. "Hear he's got some gold he's aiming to give me."

"Wait a minute, Pat. I want to talk to you before you go out there."

Pat Alder was impatient as always. "All right, talk."

Condon said, "Pat, there's something going on here that I don't understand," and he went on to tell the cattleman everything that had happened.

"So last night," he wound up, "Warner went down to the jail to talk to this Seller, and got shot."

Pat Alder grunted. "Which should prove that he isn't as guilty as you seem to think he is. A man doesn't shoot himself on purpose, even in the leg."

"He might have done it to make me think he isn't mixed up in the mess."

"You've been wearing that badge too long, boy. Never saw it to fail. Take a decent rider off the range, put a badge on him and he turns as suspicious as a badger. Why don't you take that piece of tin off and come back riding for me?"

"I might, after I clear up Cap Lennox's name."

"Uh-huh. I see. Well, come on and take me to see Warner."

"It's the fourth house on the right after you pass the corner. I'm not going back there now. Warner and I aren't too friendly this morning."

Alder started to object, then changed his mind. He went on, his shambling rider's walk making him seem clumsier than he really was.

He knocked, and when Lucy opened the door she made him blink. So this was the girl Kern had meant, the girl Joe Condon was interested in.

He said, "You're right pretty, Ma'am," and saw the color rise in her cheeks, and grinned. "I'm Pat Alder. I want to see your daddy."

She led him along the hall to a rear room where her father sat in a chair, his wounded leg stretched out in front of him.

Lloyd Warner was in a bad temper. The very idea that anyone would dare shoot him had been hard enough to accept, and Joe Condon's questions last night had been worse. To Warner this affront had been worse than the wound. By God, he ought to be above suspicion of any kind. He was the Springs' leading citizen, wasn't he? Why, damn it, he was the one who had finally okayed Condon as marshal.

Hearing a noise in the hall, he thought Condon had come back. He gathered himself for war, forming and storing up phrases with which he meant to put Condon in his place.

But it was a big, redheaded stranger who walked in. Warner had his mouth already open for a sarcastic thrust. He closed it, then opened it again to say, "Who in hell are you?"

"Pat Alder."

At once Lloyd Warner's manner changed. Pat Alder was one of the *big* ranchers. Pat Alder had ten thousand head of beef animals on the trail, by far the biggest shipment Warner would make that season. He managed a kind of wintry smile.

"Sorry, Mr. Alder. I'm laid up with a hunk of lead in my leg and I guess it's ruined my manners. Sit down."

Pat Alder sat down. He sized up the cattle buyer quickly, as he sized up all men.

"I'll start delivering into the pens day after tomorrow," he said. "I'll bring them in in bunches of a thousand. Get too many cattle in the streets and we'll all have trouble. By the time the first herd is safely delivered my foreman will be along with the second. Hope you have plenty of cars."

Warner frowned. He didn't. The railroad had been unaccountably slow in shunting them out. He did not know that Hartford Hull had held his order, purposely, so that as many cattle as possible would collect in the stock pens.

"I'll get cars," he said. "That's not your worry. I'll pay you as soon as they're tallied."

"Fair enough."

"Just make sure you get them to the stock-pens." Warner said this darkly.

"I heard you had a little trouble."

Warner exploded. "Little trouble! We've had three murders in less than three weeks and five hundred head of cattle stolen."

"I talked to Howe," Alder said. "He rode down the trail to meet me."

Warner did not express his opinion of Howe. He recalled just in time that he was talking to another Texas cattleman.

"No one's going to jump us," Pat said. "I've got too tough a crew. Besides Howe thinks the former marshal was at the head of the gang and with him dead it may have broken up."

Warner said curtly, "This morning I'm not sure that our present marshal didn't step into his shoes."

"Huh? You mean Joe Condon?" Pat Alder laughed hugely. "Joe's got his faults, but he's honest. I come close to raising him, and he hates a cattle thief more than he hates a Yankee." He stopped, remembering where he was, and laughed again.

"Well, we'll be bringing cows in, day after tomorrow, Mr. Warner. Have that gold all counted out and stacked."

He went into the hall to find Lucy waiting for him. "Don't think Father meant everything he said about Joe," she said worriedly. "His leg hurts him and his pride has suffered. Sometimes he has too much pride."

"Makes it hard on you," he said, "having him down on Condon."

"Hard on me?"

"Don't get coy with me, girl. Kern told me Joe's in love with you."

"Oh." She blushed, confused. "Your daughter told you *that?*"

"Yep. Can't fool Kern." He chuckled. "She can read a man like a book. Time was when I thought she and Joe would hit it off. Still hoped so when I came up the trail. But with you in the running, I don't know."

"But I'm not in the running. I—"

He waved it aside. "That's the stuff. Don't let Joe get too sure of you. Keep a man guessing. That's what my wife did with me and it worked out fine. We been married near thirty years." He went on down the steps and through the gate. Long after he had disappeared from view, Lucy Warner lingered on the porch, staring into space.

They must be wrong, she thought. He's never given the least sign. He was barely civil on the train.

She turned toward the door, bemused. Not until she was safely in the house did she realize with a start that she had forgotten Hartford Hull. The whole idea was absurd.

Chapter Fourteen

Pat Alder's men were dry. They had a thousand miles of trail dust packed into the back of their throats. They headed for the nearest saloon with the sure instinct of returning swallows, and Howe went along. The foreman was feeling proddy. He had vowed to come back into this town at the head of a bunch of riders who would clean out the place, and as bad luck would have it, the owner of the first herd south had turned out to be an old friend of the marshal's.

They bellied up to the bar, naming their poison, laughing as men do who have nothing particular to laugh about, but have suddenly been released from a grueling strain.

Blankton saw them come in. Blankton was sitting in a poker game at one of the rear tables. There were two house men in the game, and two merchants. The play was small, merely a time-killing operation, and Blankton felt bored and ready to pull out.

Both of Alder's men had money in their pockets, the first money they had seen in months, and it was burning its way through the frayed cloth.

Ned Martin got into the game first, then when Blankton quit Alf Hudson took his seat. Blankton retreated to the far end of the bar, one eye on the game, the other on Howe. He had recognized Howe at once, guessed that he was in a bad mood, and smelled trouble.

He did not know the men with Howe and he did not care. Their shaggy hair, their burned faces and their worn clothes marked them as trail riders as plainly as if it had been tattooed on their foreheads.

The game went on. Howe was getting drunk, standing hunched by himself, staring moodily at the backbar mirror.

And then one of the house men made a mistake. The pot was fairly large, nearly forty dollars. He was dealing. He had given Ned Martin three queens, and on the draw he dealt his partner a third ace. He did it purposely because he knew Blankton was watching and Frenchy Talbert had promised him a thousand dollars if the law closed this saloon for running a crooked game. He did it clumsily so that Blankton could see him, but Ned Martin saw it also, and that was the mistake.

Ned kicked back his chair. His right hand snaked out and caught the gambler's wrist while his left cut across in a sweeping curve to crash against the side of the house man's head.

"You damn tinhorn," Martin roared.

Even then there might not have been fireworks. The sprawled gambler did not mean to go for his holdout gun. All he wanted was enough trouble to enable him to collect from Frenchy. The second house man sat frozen, palms down on the table top, out of the play.

Ned Martin pulled his iron. He was breathing deeply, looking for someone to shoot at, when Blankton's voice cut at him.

"Put it away, cowboy."

Martin swiveled his head toward the bar. Blankton's gun was in his hand, and his eyes were glittering. "Put it away," Blankton said.

Martin would have to make a half turn to hit Blankton. He stood there, weighing his chances. Alf Hudson sat with his back to the marshal. He had not even drawn.

It was a stand-off and Martin knew it. He said in an aggrieved voice, "He cheated. He pulled an ace from the bottom."

"I know it. I saw him." Blankton took a step away from the bar. He had forgotten Howe, and of such oversights tragedies are made. Through Howe's whiskey-dimmed senses there filtered the single fact that an honest range rider had locked horns with one of those ornery crooked marshals. He pulled his gun.

The bartender's startled cry warned Blankton. He spun, deadly as a striking snake. His heavy slug caught Howe directly in the stomach, even as Howe's finger tightened on his trigger. His shot went wild, digging into the splintered floor at Blankton's feet, but Blankton never saw it. He whirled around again just as Ned Martin fired. The bullet cut Blankton's shirt between his side and arm. And then he killed Ned Martin with a single shot between the eyes.

The room became very, very still. No one moved. The gambler who had caused the trouble still lay sprawled on his back. The second house man and Alf Hudson still sat in their places, like figures in a waxworks.

The bar's owner, a man named Jacks, introduced the first motion by slamming back the office door and plunging into the room. He saw Martin on the floor, and Blankton with the gun still in his hand, and Howe sprawled in front of the bar.

"My God," he whispered hoarsely. The bar was not as large as the Western Belle, yet Jacks had enjoyed a good, steady play, and he knew that this might well put him out of business.

"Why did you do that?" His whisper had become a wail.

Blankton did not look at him. He walked over to the card table, still carrying the gun in his hand, and stirred the prostrate gambler with his toe. "Get up," he said.

The man obeyed him. Alf Hudson seemed to be coming out of a deep fog. He was not a quick-witted man and things had happened much too fast for him to follow. He got up slowly, and for a long moment he stood looking down at the body of his partner. Then his face contorted with shock and rage.

"You damn butcher," he snarled at Blankton. "What did you want to kill him for?"

Blankton's face was wooden. He didn't even seem to hear. "Give me your gun," he said.

Hudson stared at him.

"Pull it slow and reverse it, cowboy."

Hudson obeyed as if his muscles were acting with no dictate from his brain.

"Get over against the wall and stay there," Blankton said.

He obeyed, sinking into a daze again, and Blankton forgot him. He could afford to; obviously there was little danger in Alf Hudson. He turned to Jacks.

"Your man cheated," he said.

Jacks looked at the dealer.

"He cheated," Blankton said. "I saw him. So did that jasper." He jerked his head toward Hudson. "You know the rule, Jacks."

Jacks's round face went white. "Now wait." His voice had a quaver in it, partly anger, partly helplessness. "It ain't my fault. I gave strict orders." He appealed to the second house man. "Didn't I give strict orders? Didn't I?"

"Close your doors," Blankton said.

Jacks's face went from white to red, then, and anger deepened his voice. "You can't shut me up like this and you know it. I've got a right to a hearing. I've got a right—"

"Never mind your rights. What's going on?"

It was Joe Condon. He had been a full block up the street when he heard the first shot, and he had beaten the curious to the saloon door by a dozen steps. They crowded in now, surging forward as those behind tried to push in to see.

"Get out," Condon told them. "Get out, all of you. Stay on the sidewalk."

They went reluctantly. He followed them, shutting the storm door. Then he walked back into the room. He saw Ned Martin on the floor and a stab of pain took him. Of all the Box A crew he and Ned had been closest. They had shared blankets, and fought storms and brush. His eyes shifted, fleetingly touching Howe's crumpled form and then centered on Blankton.

"What happened?"

There was a trace of defiance in Blankton's manner. Not that he felt any guilt. He had done what had to be done according to his lights and the fact that he had derived momentary pleasure from gunplay had nothing to do with it.

He described exactly what had happened from the moment the Box A riders entered the saloon. "They were wearing guns," he said. "I should have called them when they first came in. I didn't." It was as near to an apology as he would ever make. "This dealer cheated and he called him." Blankton pointed to Martin's still body. "But there wouldn't have been any trouble if Howe hadn't been liquored."

Joe Condon said in a low voice, "Did you have to shoot Ned?"

Blankton guessed that the rider on the floor was named Ned. He said simply, "He shot at me," and exhibited the tear in his shirt.

Condon felt a little sick at his stomach. Jacks chose this moment to horn in.

"It wasn't my fault if he cheated, Marshal. You can't close me."

Condon turned on him with unaccustomed savagery. "If it wasn't for your lousy place two good men would still be alive. You're closed, and you'll stay closed, and if you're still in town when tomorrow's train leaves, I'll personally hound you until you wish you'd never been born. Now get out of my way."

He intended to summon the doctor who doubled as coroner, but a disturbance outside the saloon stopped him. The doors flapped violently and Pat Alder came charging in with all the grace of a huge untamed bull. He dominated the place immediately, just by existing. He stopped. He saw Ned Martin's twisted body.

"What happened?"

Joe Condon felt the power of the rancher. He had taken orders from this man for nearly a dozen years, and the pull of authority was strong.

He told it exactly as Blankton had told it to him. Pat listened, his wind-scorched face gaining a deeper shade. "So Ned got cheated and when he squawked he got shot."

"It wasn't quite like that," Joe Condon said evenly. "Ned made two mistakes. He shouldn't have worn a gun in town, and he shouldn't have shot at my deputy. Blankton's badge was in plain sight. The order he gave was clear."

Pat Alder lumbered about and eyed Blankton. Blankton had retreated until he stood with his back against the bar, facing the room. He seemed to know he was on trial, and he wanted to be ready to defend himself if the verdict went against him.

After a long look, which would place Blankton's face in his memory for future reference, Alder clumped ponderously over to Alf Hudson.

"How was it, Alf?"

Alf's voice was wavery, but his rage had been building all this while.

"He cut him down like a damn butcher, Pat. He didn't have no call to shoot."

Joe Condon knew his former employer thoroughly. He saw the lumps and ridges of muscle under Pat's shirt tighten. He said, "In a way Howe started it. If he hadn't been drunk and pulled a gun there wouldn't have been any trouble."

Pat Alder spun like a giant top. "If this town didn't harbor tinhorns and card sharks there wouldn't have been any trouble. Howe tried to tell me. Howe rode into my camp asking help, and when I heard you were the marshal I turned him down. What's the matter with you, Joe? Have you forgotten the men you were raised with?"

"No one in the world can feel worse about Ned Martin's death than I do, Pat. But just as you back your men, I back mine. Blankton was doing what he had to do."

"He was doing what the easy money these gamblers are paying you made him do."

Condon sighed. "If that's the way you want it, Pat—"

"That's the way it is," Alder rumbled ominously, and knowing the big man's sudden rages, Joe Condon was afraid that Alder would go for his gun.

He wasn't afraid for himself, but for the belligerent giant. Blankton stood on Alder's right, and Blankton's eyes were hot. If Pat Alder's hand moved, he was dead.

Perhaps Alder sensed this. Perhaps even in his deep rage he could not bring himself to draw against the man he had practically raised. At any rate he said, "When the crew gets here, Joe, keep out of the way—and keep him out of my sight." He jerked his thumb toward Blankton.

Blankton's attitude did not change. He still suggested a hungry wolf, ready to spring, but he turned away, showing his back, hooking his elbows on the bar, letting negligence express his contempt for the rancher's threat.

Pat Alder glanced at Alf Hudson. He made a small sign with his hand. Then he went toward the doors with Hudson hurrying at his heels, like a small terrier that is fearful of being left behind.

They pushed their way through the crowd which packed the door and vanished onto the street.

Condon sent the bartender to bring the doctor. After that he walked over to Blankton. Blankton said, "Thanks, Joe."

"For what?"

"For not backing down before that hell-hound."

"If you were right I shouldn't have backed down."

"I was right."

"You might have shot a leg out from under him."

"And got myself killed doing it? No dice. When I use a gun I use it for keeps."

Condon did not push it. There seemed to be nothing more to say. Ned Martin was dead, just as Cap Lennox was dead, and Pete Ortman. The whole thing filled him with a growing distaste. He wished fervently now that he had turned in his badge and left the Springs before this happened, but he was not a man to waste time on useless regrets.

He strode toward Jacks, who was standing sullenly in the corner. "Clean out your office and pay off your men," he said.

Jacks gulped and shook his head hopelessly. "You mean it, don't you?"

"I mean it."

"You're a hard man, Condon. What about my lease? What about my stock?"

"You should have thought of that before you ran a crooked game."

"I gave orders to play it straight. Ask the bartender. Someone crossed me."

Condon stared at him hard. "Why should anyone do that?"

Jacks spread his hands in a gesture of futility. "How should I know? Maybe I've got an enemy. Maybe somebody was trying to put me out of business."

"They succeeded," Condon said. He went back to Blankton, saying in a low voice, "What's the house man's name—the one who started this?"

"Al Yale. Shall I lock him up?"

"No." Condon frowned. "I've got an idea maybe Jacks is telling the truth."

"You mean you're going to let him stay?"

"No. He closes. But I want you to keep an eye on Yale. See where he goes, who he talks to, and if he comes up with an extra amount of money."

“And if he tries to leave town?”

“Run him in. I’m going to get to the bottom of this whole business if I have to close every joint in town.”

Chapter Fifteen

Jerome Boyce had never desired to be mayor of Dexter Springs. The honor had come to him because of two people, Lloyd Warner and Boyce's wife. Warner had picked him because he mistook Boyce's mildness of manner for weakness and felt certain that he could control the man.

Mrs. Boyce's motives were more complex. All her drab, colorless life she had dreamed of honors, of being important, of having people envy her. She was flattered by Warner's suggestion and she helped bully her husband into accepting the office.

Boyce had not liked it from the first and he liked it less now as he opened Warner's front gate and climbed the porch steps to knock on the door.

He had been summoned to an emergency meeting of the council, and since Warner's leg wound handicapped him the meeting was being held at his house.

Boyce knew what the meeting was about. The town had been talking of little else since the shooting that afternoon. He knocked a second time and waited. The door opened and he saw the girl outlined in the semi-darkness of the hall. Then he said in his quiet voice, "Has the clan already gathered, Lucy?"

She laughed, but the laughter held a note of strain. "They're all here, Mayor, sharpening their knives for Joe Condon."

He said, "As bad as that?" He liked this quiet girl, understanding her far better than her father did, appreciating her good sense and her depth of character.

"You won't let them hang him?" She was still trying to speak lightly, but the urgency broke through. He looked at her in surprise.

"I didn't know you were so friendly with Condon."

"I'm not," she said quickly, perhaps too quickly. "But it seems to me that a man who's trying to do his job the way he is should have support. They're all worried because that cowboy got killed and Pat Alder is raging mad. He spent an hour with my father this afternoon, threatening to send word down the trail for the herds to stay out of the Springs."

"I know. He came to see me."

"They all think more of a dollar than what is right," she said indignantly. "Even Hartford thinks something should be done to Blankton. He and Joe are arguing now."

Boyce went along the hall, wincing at the loud voices from the rear room, conscious that the girl was following him. He paused in the open doorway. All five of the council members were indeed present.

Warner sat with his wounded leg propped on a hassock. Joe Condon presented his back to the door as he argued with Hull and Bill Gilmore.

Condon was saying, "I'll turn in my badge before I fire Blankton. What would any of you have done if you'd been caught in the same circumstances? Two men shooting at you?"

"That might be a good idea." Warner spoke from his chair, his cold voice more chilly than usual. "To turn in your badge, I mean. There's been nothing but trouble ever since you took over. You've demonstrated that you cannot control the town."

Condon looked at him with open dislike.

"I'll be glad to," he said, "as soon as the last Box A steer is shipped, and as soon as the last of Alder's riders are on their way back down the trail."

Hartford Hull watched him as he spoke. Hull thought himself unobserved and he could not keep all the satisfaction from his face. Things could not be working out any better. The Western Belle's largest rival had closed. Alder and his men would be so hostile to the marshal that there was little danger of their joining forces with him no matter what happened, and the town was rapidly becoming alienated from Condon.

He said, "Why wait that long, Joe?"

Condon studied him, sensing a shift in Hull's attitude toward him without being quite able to identify it. "I'll tell you why," he said, and addressed the whole room. "Most of you probably think what's happened in the last few days is a series of unrelated accidents. Well, you are wrong. I don't know who planned things, or who expects to gain by them, but I'm going to find out."

They stared at him, Warner in anger, Hull in quickened curiosity, the rest a little puzzled. Hull said, "Surely you aren't implying that what happened this afternoon was planned, that Blankton deliberately arranged things in order to shoot those two men?"

Joe Condon shook his head. He was not used to debate, to trying to explain his actions or the actions of others. Only deep anger, and deeper concern, held him in the room.

"Blankton planned nothing," he said. "But someone was very careful to set the stage. Yale, the dealer who cheated and caused all the trouble, went directly from Jacks's place to the Western Belle."

"What has that got to do with it?"

"Yale went into Frenchy Talbert's office. He came out twenty minutes later and went to the house where he boards. When we arrested him he was packing his things and he had one thousand dollars in cash in his pocket. He was leaving town."

"What does that prove?" Hull said in a dry

voice. "A man gets into trouble, naturally he wants to leave town. The money in his pocket proves nothing. He could have saved it."

Condon said, "That wasn't the attitude any of you took when money was found on Cap Lennox. You tried him in your minds, and you found him guilty."

Hull's face reddened. Warner said sharply, "It seems to me that you might at least have questioned him."

"I did," Condon said, and he grinned faintly at the memory. "I might even have gotten a little rough, because he talked. He said Frenchy Talbert offered him one thousand dollars if he cheated in a game and got caught."

"Got caught?" Warner exploded. "This is crazy. Why should Talbert want him to get caught?"

"So Jacks's place would be closed. So Talbert could knock out competition."

"I've never heard such a silly idea in my life," Warner said. "A move like this can't help Talbert. How does he know the play won't go to one of the other saloons? How does he know someone won't reopen Jacks's place next week?"

"I agree that it won't help Talbert," Joe Condon said pleasantly. "We closed him half an hour ago."

Hull could not believe his ears. "You closed the Western Belle?"

"That's right." Condon was beginning to enjoy himself.

"But what did Talbert do?"

"He didn't do anything. He's in jail."

Lloyd Warner said grimly, "It begins to sound as if you intend to jail the whole town."

"I will if I have to. I'll close every saloon along Railroad Avenue. I'm going to have no trouble here as long as the Box A crew is in the country. I know Pat Alder. He and his men are going to ride in here with blood in their eyes, looking for a fight. I'm not going to give them an excuse."

"You'll give them nothing!" Warner shouted. "You're fired!"

Jerome Boyce had been standing just inside the doorway, taking no part in the conversation. Now he made his bid.

"I think Condon makes a lot of sense," he said quietly. "We have a bad situation here and it isn't of his making. Fire him and what do you use for a marshal? Certainly not Blankton. Alder's crew would shoot him on sight. Do any of you want to strap on a gun and take over until we can import someone?"

They sat there in silence, balked by facts. Even Lloyd Warner shut up and listened.

Boyce's tone became a little more brisk. "Personally I think Joe is doing a good job in a hard spot. Personally I'd hate to see him leave, and I'd like to point out one thing to you, Lloyd. Under our town charter the mayor does the hiring and firing of a marshal. And I'm still mayor."

Behind him, Lucy Warner made a small approving noise. Her father did not share her pleasure. This was unexpected mutiny. He opened his mouth to protest, then closed it slowly. For once in his life Lloyd Warner had nothing to say.

Later, on the dark porch with Hartford Hull, Lucy laughed softly. "Did you ever see anything as funny as Father's face? You'd have thought Mr. Boyce had stabbed him in the back."

Hull was abstracted. Ordinarily his quick mind met each situation almost before it arose and solved a problem before it developed. But he had never even considered the possibility that Condon might close the Western Belle, or arrest Frenchy Talbert.

He needed Talbert, needed him free. Since Hull had never appeared openly in any of their ventures, he did not even know most of the men who had conducted the cattle raid.

Talbert had to be free by the time the Box A steers were delivered to the cattle pens. He had to be free to organize the raid, and to arrange for Pat Alder to be waylaid on his ride back to the Nations with the gold.

He answered Lucy with only half his mind and she caught his inattention. She said, "You didn't support Condon tonight."

"Joe makes mistakes like everyone else," he told her lightly. "He had no right to close the Western Belle on nothing more than this Yale's word. Don't forget I run a newspaper, and a newspaper depends on advertisers."

Her voice sharpened. "Are you taking the same position my father takes—that anything is all right as long as you make money?"

"Now, Lucy, you know that isn't true."

She studied him in the half light, realizing in a kind of surprise how very little she did know about him or his inner thoughts. Most of the things she had found to admire in him were surface qualities.

She said suddenly, "What of the future, Hartford? What do you plan to do when you leave Dexter?"

He started, half guiltily, for he had had no idea that she suspected he meant to leave the Springs. "What makes you ask that? Why should I even think of leaving here?"

"I hear talk," she said. "People say that after this season the Springs will no longer be a shipping point. And what else is there? Some day I suppose the country around here will be settled up and this will be a trading center, but it isn't now."

He said, "Stop worrying your pretty head about such matters. I'll make the plans."

It was an order, and Lucy Warner did not

like orders. She said quietly, "It's my life too, remember. Don't try to shut me out the way my father shut out my mother. I want to share things. A marriage should be a partnership."

He felt harried. "Look, Lucy, this isn't the time to make plans. The paper comes out again tomorrow, and we have more news to publish than we have had in months."

"I'm not trying to be tiresome," she said, a little stubbornly. "But every time I try to talk with you, you put me off. Don't ever try to shut me out, or I won't be around when you come back."

They were closer to a fight that they had ever been, and he knew a quick annoyance with her. Damn it, women had no real part in a man's life. They were necessary for certain things, but they should be relegated to the background and kept there.

He said, "I didn't mean to shut you out. I'm worried. Things are not going well in town and with your father laid up it means I have to do double duty. We'll talk again when there's more time."

He kissed her then. He held her tightly in his arms and whispered softly against her hair, and then he let her go and went away, leaving her silent and dissatisfied in the darkness.

He went directly to the marshal's office, speaking to several men whom he passed but not pausing until he walked into the lighted room.

Joe Condon and Blankton were there, and he got the impression that they had been arguing before he came in.

During the short walk from the house he had recovered his poise, and he managed to smile as he said, "More trouble?"

Condon looked him over carefully. He kept remembering the change in Hull's manner during the council meeting, but he found no trace of it now. Hull seemed his usual affable self.

"No trouble," Condon said. "I was just telling Blankton that I'm going to send him to the state capital until after the Box A leaves this part of the country."

"Good idea," Hull agreed promptly. "We don't want any more trouble than we have to have."

Blankton's face was set in a stubborn cast. "I'm not going. I never ran from anyone and I'm not running now."

Hull considered. Having Blankton out of town could well help his plans. The man was an experienced fighter, and when it came time to raid the stock in the pens beside the railroad tracks he would be an added threat.

"It isn't a question of running away," he said. "No one doubts your courage. Joe can think up some business at the state capital, and it's perfectly natural that he should send you."

"I'm not going."

Hull shrugged. The point was of minor importance, really. He had a number of other things to engage his attention. He turned to Condon.

"The paper comes out this morning."

Condon did not sound interested. "I know it."

"There will be a lot of news. I want Blankton's story of the fight, how it started and what he did."

"No."

Hull frowned at Condon, exasperated. "Now listen, Joe. This is news and you have no business trying to suppress news. If you do, people will wonder. They'll gossip, and—"

"Let them."

Hull sighed. Then he adopted the tone of a teacher enlightening a backward schoolboy. "Joe, please understand. You're a public officer and you can't ignore the people. If you don't tell your side of a story they'll make one up for you, and it won't be in your favor."

Condon said, "I want nothing printed in the paper. The more this is publicized the worse it will get. If I can get Blankton out of town before Pat's men ride in, I can handle things. But if there are copies of the paper lying around, telling Blankton's story, it will fire their tempers all over again. The answer is no."

Hull groaned dramatically. "Boy, do you make it hard for a man. All right, if I can't talk to Blankton, let me talk to Frenchy Talbert and that man Yale. The news that the Western Belle is closed demands some explanation."

"No."

This second refusal really disturbed Hull. He had to talk to Talbert. It was absolutely necessary that he find out exactly what arrangements Talbert had already made and the only way to do it was to see him under the guise of an interview.

He tried sarcasm. "Surely you don't think an interview with a saloon man whose place has been closed will do you any harm with Alder? To my mind it would do just the opposite. It would show your former boss that you're trying to clean up the town to protect his men."

"I wasn't thinking about Alder."

"Then why can't I interview him?"

"Because," Condon said, "if someone north of the tracks is behind Talbert, that man is already beginning to sweat. I want him to sweat. I want him to worry about what is happening to Talbert. I want him to worry so much that he will show his hand."

"I see," Hull said slowly. "That makes a kind of sense."

"In a poker game," Condon said, "you keep pressure on the other fellow if you can. The same should work here."

Hull shrugged. "I can't argue with you, and I wouldn't if I could." He moved toward the door. "Maybe I can help you in the way I write the story of the arrest." He went out and paused on the dark street, thinking, trying to plan. He was not exactly worried, but this meant complications. One thing was certain. He had already made up his mind to it. Joe Condon had to die.

Chapter Sixteen

Joe Condon came out of the marshal's office, carrying a folded copy of the *Sentinel* under his arm. He was as thoroughly angry as a man can be.

Hartford Hull had devoted the full front page of the paper to the story of the gunfight, the arrest of Yale, the closing of the Western Belle and the arrest of Frenchy Talbert.

Not only that, but in a two-column editorial he had reviewed everything that had happened since Cap Lennox's murder. But it was the closing paragraphs of Hull's editorial which had raised Condon's ire:

> Every citizen of Dexter Springs must be aware that this town's whole survival depends upon the herds which come up the long trail from Texas, and on the good will of the men who bring those herds. Yet our new marshal seems to be doing his best to alienate these very men.
>
> I was responsible for this man's appointment, and I now ask for his removal. If he has his way he will close every establishment south of Railroad Avenue. He will arrest every trail rider as

> he comes into town. Every member of the Council with the exception of our mayor agrees with me. I therefore call upon all citizens to help, to take up the cause. I demand a new deal in the marshal's office. I demand the arrest of the deputy who caused two deaths yesterday and who, if not checked, can well cause more.
>
> To arms! This is no time for men to hesitate. If our government has failed to function, then it is time for a committee of citizens to take over . . .

Condon marched down the street and into the newspaper office. Hull was not there. The printer wiped his mouth with the back of an ink-stained hand and spat into a battered can.

"Ain't seen him all morning, Marshal."

Condon sensed that the man was laughing at him behind the mask of his dirty face. He turned on his heel and left the office. It occurred to him that Hull was hiding, and then he dismissed the thought with a shrug. Hartford Hull, whatever else his faults, was not a coward.

Condon passed a dozen men on the street. They all spoke to him, but there was a definite change in their attitude, a reserved quality which had not existed before, as if they were holding themselves withdrawn until they could make up their minds.

He came to the hardware store which Jerome

Boyce operated and went in. A woman was buying a coil of small rope and talking vehemently to the mayor as she completed her purchase. She saw Condon and her flow of words stopped abruptly. She accepted her change and scurried from the store as if the air had suddenly become unbreathable.

Boyce made a mild clucking noise, then turned to Condon. Surprisingly he winked.

Condon moved over to the counter and laid down the newspaper. "I suppose you've seen this?"

The little mayor nodded. "Good writer, Hartford. Makes the words go together real nice."

"Look," Condon said. "I appreciate your backing me, but you seem to be about the only one who is. You're in business in this town and you have to live with these people." He reached up to unpin the badge from his shirt.

Boyce said, "I didn't think you were a quitter, son."

Condon let his hand fall to his side. "Say that again."

Boyce smiled, a small, twisting smile. "I've lived a mite longer than you have," he said, "and I've probably seen a right smart larger number of people. People get stirred up, and that's Hartford's job, to stir them up. I'll bet he sold more papers this morning than he ever will again."

"He's playing with fire," Condon said.

"Sure. But he isn't the one who gets burned."

"Then you think he wrote that merely to sell papers?"

"And advertising. Don't forget that a lot of the men south of the tracks carry ads in his paper. They figure that Pete Ortman and Frenchy Talbert were big, powerful men. If Ortman can be killed and Talbert arrested and closed, they don't know what will happen to them."

"Then you don't think Hull was ordered to write as he did?"

Boyce squinted at him over his square, steel-rimmed glasses. "Ordered, by whom?"

Condon did not know. He certainly did not want to mention Warner's name. He said, "It doesn't matter. The thing is, he did write it. He did stir up this town as it's never been stirred up before, and it's going to make things twice as hard when Alder rides in."

Boyce said, "Why don't you ride out and talk to Alder? He was riled yesterday. He might have calmed down some today."

Joe Condon did not believe this. He had known Pat Alder too long to believe that anything would ever calm the rancher down, but he could not very well refuse.

"I hate to leave town," he said. "I hate to let Blankton step out onto the street alone. Some fool will probably take a shot at him if he does."

Boyce shrugged. "You can't be everywhere, Joe. Just tell Blankton to watch himself."

"I already have. He won't listen. He thinks someone will take it that he's afraid."

The little storekeeper sighed. "The trouble with men is pride. Half of them would stay clear of trouble if it wasn't for their pride. Well, you and I can't change things. We'll just have to do the best we can."

Leaving the store, Condon had a warm feeling for the little man. Not since Cap Lennox's death had he felt like this about anyone in Dexter Springs. Also, he realized something which he had not suspected before—that Boyce and the dead marshal had certain traits in common. They were honest, and they did not back away from anything.

He debated going back to the marshal's office to warn Blankton again about staying off the street, and decided not to do it. He headed toward the livery stable where he kept his horse. Just before he reached the runway entrance, Lucy Warner came around the corner of the side street beyond the building.

"It's nice to see you," he said. "It turns a bad morning into a good one."

For once, she did not smile. Her face remained grave, her eyes shadowed. "You've seen the paper?"

He said, "Of course," and the morning seemed bad again.

"Have you talked to Hartford?"

He shook his head.

"I've been trying to find him," she said, and she sounded angry. "I simply can't believe that he did it."

Condon's shrug was slight but expressive. "Sometimes we aren't always our own bosses, Lucy."

"What do you mean by that?"

He hesitated. He had no desire to discuss Hull with anyone, especially this girl whom Hull was supposed to marry. "I guess I didn't mean much of anything," he said. "I've got to ride out and try and talk some sense into Pat Alder's hard head."

"I wish I could go with you," she said impulsively. "I've never seen a trail herd on the move. For that matter I've never seen very much of this country."

"Why don't you?" He spoke on impulse too. "I can get a buckboard. We'll be back before dark."

She started to refuse. She knew Hull would not approve, but the very thought of Hull changed her decision.

"Why not, if we can stop by the house for a few minutes."

They went on into the stable, and already Joe Condon had begun to regret the invitation. She belonged to Hull, and he must guard his tongue constantly.

But as he swung the buckboard into the broad hoof-marked trace which led southeastward, he found that there could be satisfaction in just riding at her side, feeling her light body jounce against him as the red wheels struck a hump in the road, listening to her talk, easy and unrestrained.

"I like it." She was gazing out across the rolling hills. "It's funny, but I've hardly been out of the Springs since we moved here. Hartford says there's no place to go. It never occurs to him that it's fun just to ride in the sunshine, just to be alive."

He laughed.

"Did you and Kern ride a lot?"

"We were crazy kids," he said. "We thought nothing of riding a hundred miles to a dance."

She sighed. "It's strange how different people's lives are. I don't think I've been to more than four or five dances in my life. Father never approved and Hartford thought they were a waste of time."

"I'll take you," he said, without thinking. "Next time the firemen throw their dance. We'll show them how it's done."

She gave him a small smile. "Do you think that would be wise?"

He felt a sudden, welling urge to catch her in his arms, to hold her with his strength, to force his mouth against hers, to tell her that he loved her as Hartford Hull could never love her. But some inner wall of conscience which was stronger than desire held him back.

"Sometimes I get tired of being wise," he said.

She sensed the strain beneath his words and was startled by her own awareness. She tried to shift the conversation.

"What will you do when you leave the Springs?" she asked breathlessly. "Surely you won't be content to wear a marshal's badge all your life?"

He looked off across the hills, steadying his emotions. No one had ever stirred him as this girl had. Even with the violence of desire coursing through him, he sensed her quiet depth, her steadfastness and loyalty. This was a girl with whom a man could plan an ordered life, a future rich with companionship and common enjoyment.

"I want a ranch," he said. "Something that's mine, that I've built myself. I want it north somewhere, new country without the feuds and bitterness which still linger in Texas, born of the war. I guess what I'm looking for is peace. I've seen a lot of fighting and I'm tired of it. Fighting always means defeat for someone."

She knew when to be silent, too. She waited, understanding him better, seeing a boy who had gone away to war and come back a man, only to find no peace.

"I want a place to raise my family," he went on, speaking now more to himself than to her. He had never really put his hopes for the future into words before.

"Your family?"

He reddened, and his laugh was shaky and embarrassed. "I suppose every man wants a family, someone to carry on his name, although a lot of men won't admit it."

She decided to take a chance. "With Kern?"

"Definitely *not* with Kern. Kern has her points—beauty, brains and a ruthless drive—but trying to live with Kern is like trying to ride an unbroken horse. Just when you think you know exactly where she's going she changes direction. No, when I marry, if I ever do, it will be some girl who loves the land, who will work, and put up with hardships and disappointments and bad times to help build something permanent and lasting. Someone I can talk to, who will want to share the problems and help make the decisions."

"That sounds wonderful," she said hesitantly. "So few men consider that women have brains enough to do more than cook and wash dishes and sweep the floor."

All the wistfulness, the longing, the deep hunger in her reached out and touched him. They looked at each other, and suddenly, without another word being spoken, she was in his arms and he was kissing her fiercely.

But after the first passionate response she drew away, not fighting him, but not returning his caress.

"Lucy?"

"Please—I've got to think."

"What's there to think about? This had to happen. I love you. I've loved you from almost the first time I saw you. It's what kept me in town. It's why I haven't pulled out before now."

"There's Hartford."

He knew a great violence, a surging desire to say, "To hell with Hartford. To hell with everything but us." But he checked himself. A wrong word now might alter her mood. At least he had hope. He had waited without hope for so long. He could wait longer with it.

He glanced around the horizon, steadying himself, giving Lucy a moment to collect herself. He saw dust, kicked up far behind them by two riders, and wondered idly who they were.

If he had not been so engrossed with Lucy he might have noticed them before. They had been following him ever since he left town.

Chapter Seventeen

Blankton was restless. He stood at the window of the marshal's office, staring bleakly out at the street, brooding darkly about Hartford Hull's editorial. Curiously he did not feel the deep rage at the newspaper man which had been Joe Condon's reaction, but he did imagine that people all over town thought he was hiding, cooped up here in the city hall.

Phil Moore and Blankton's younger brother Harvey were out on the street. He wished one of them would come in and relieve him. To hell with what Condon had said. He was not going to stay out of sight. He would show the town he was not afraid of anything or anybody.

Finally he could stand the inactivity no longer. He called through the window to a boy and sent him to track down either Harvey or Moore.

Half an hour later, Moore came in.

"I been in here long enough," Blankton said. "You stay and play nursemaid to the prisoners."

"But Condon said—"

"Condon isn't God."

Phil Moore was troubled. He did not actually like Blankton, but he considered the older man to be an ally in adversity. In his mind, both had been put upon, both had gotten a poor deal.

"I don't know," Moore said. "The town is fairly stirred up. Half a dozen gamblers tried to ride me a while ago. I just walked away."

"I won't walk away," Blankton said. "When the rats see me they'll run for their holes."

After that he walked out.

Phil Moore slouched over to the window and watched him stride around the corner. Then he came back to the desk. A voice from the jail wing called his name. He grumbled to himself, but he went to the grill which separated the office from the jail corridor, and unlocked it.

"What's the matter?"

Frenchy Talbert was in the end cell, the one in which Sam Seller had been killed. "Come here a minute, Moore. I want to talk to you."

Phil Moore did not move.

"What's the matter?" Talbert said in a mocking voice. "You scared?"

Moore came forward. He swaggered as he came, but his laugh sounded empty. "Why should I be afraid of a man who's locked up?"

"I won't be locked up for long."

"That's what you say, big man."

That rasped on Talbert. He was used to having people like Moore try to curry his favor. He said, "Listen, kid, you haven't got many brains, but use the few you have. You saw the paper this morning. Condon is through, and that fool mayor is through too, for siding him. I have friends. If you don't believe it, how do you think I moved into the Western Belle after Pete was killed?"

In spite of himself Phil Moore was impressed. All his short life he had taken orders from people in authority and the shakiness of Condon's position worried him deeply.

"I never did anything to you, Frenchy," he said in the tone of a man asking for a truce.

Talbert smiled to himself. He was an old hand at pushing venal public officials. "You never did anything for me, either. I've got to get out of here."

"No." The very idea horrified Phil Moore. "Condon would kill me."

"Look," Talbert said. "It's only a matter of hours until Condon won't be marshal any more. And Blankton's going to get killed on the street. You can be sure of that."

Phil Moore gulped. Talbert sure made it sound final.

"Who will be marshal then?" Frenchy Talbert asked.

Phil Moore thought about it. He had to. With Blankton and Condon out of the way, he would be next in line. "I don't know," he said thickly. His mouth was cotton dry.

"You can be, if you play it smart. Look, all you have to do is stand close to the door. I reach out and grab your gun. No one is going to blame you if you open the door when you have a gun on you."

"I'd look like a fool."

"You'll look like a worse fool if you don't. Who do you suppose runs this town, anyway? You read the paper this morning. Why do you suppose Hull wrote the way he did?"

Phil Moore did not know. He did not dare to guess, either.

"Because the big augur told him to. When a man like Hull takes orders, what about you?"

Still Moore could think of nothing to say.

"Here." Talbert reached in his inside pocket. "At least Condon didn't take my money. I've got five hundred here." He held it up for Moore to see, careful not to extend it between the bars. "This is only the first payment. There's a lot more where it came from. If you play it right you can be the biggest man in Dexter Springs."

Phil Moore was only twenty-one. He had never even held one hundred dollars in his hand. Not all in one sheaf, not all at one time.

His eyes lit hungrily. He wavered, and then he advanced slowly toward the cell door, one hand extended. Talbert watched him like a rattler watching a desert mouse. When the extended hand was within inches of the bars, Talbert's hand shot through. His fingers locked about Phil Moore's wrist and he jerked the deputy against the bars. Moore's head struck the grille with enough force to stun him.

For an instant he wobbled there, dazed, and in that instant Frenchy's left hand snaked the heavy gun from his holster. The next thing Phil Moore knew, the muzzle of the gun was prodding him in the stomach.

"All right, open it up."

Moore tried to gather his wits. He thought of grabbing Talbert's wrist and banging it against the bars hard enough to dislodge the gun. But Talbert stepped back just in time, still covering him.

"Open up, boy."

He unlocked the door. Talbert darted through, quick as a cat. He brought the heavy gun up and slammed it down across Phil Moore's head. Moore dropped without a sound.

"Chump," Frenchy Talbert said, and then he crossed to the opposite cell and released Yale.

The gambler came out babbling thanks.

"Get out of town," Talbert said coldly. "If you're caught again I'll have you killed."

The man's face went blank. He stood for an instant without speaking. "I hope they hang you," he said, and bolted down the corridor.

Talbert gave him no second thought. He stuffed Moore's gun into his waistband and walked casually from the office. On Second Street he met two men who knew him. They stopped and stared. He nodded, a twisting, sarcastic smile on his dark, handsome face, sauntering by them with no apparent concern.

At the corner of Railroad Avenue he stopped to scan the street's dusty length. He saw Blankton's tall figure a full block away. For the first time since he had left the jail, Talbert hesitated. Then he darted across the tracks and lost himself in the maze of alleys to the south.

Blankton had not seen him. Blankton's progress along the street which divided the upper part of town from the saloon district had been slow and studied. He had hit every place in the line, stalking into the long, dark, smoky rooms with their perpetual odors of spilled beer, cheap whiskey and unwashed bodies, walking as far as the end of the bar to give a slow, raking, examining look, and then turning deliberately, presenting his back as if in invitation for attack.

But for all that, it was beginning to tell on him. Each step he took in leaving was a painful uncertainty. Each time he entered a new saloon it took more will power, and the news of his coming always flashed ahead of him down the row.

He reached Kirk Aminstead's place. It was the last place in the whole town in which he expected trouble. Kirk was as near a friend as Blankton could claim among the men along the south side of Railroad Avenue.

He stepped in, saw Kirk behind the bar, and

relaxed. But before he reached the high, scarred counter, his sixth sense warned him of tension.

The room was fairly small, not half the size of the Western Belle, yet there were more men present than he had seen in any saloon that morning.

Blankton recognized most of them without knowing their names—gamblers from a dozen different spots along the street, hangers-on without visible means of support who nevertheless continued to make the Springs their headquarters.

He looked at Kirk. "What is this?" he said.

The saloon man bent to get a bottle, saying in a tone which carried the words only to Blankton's ears, "You shouldn't have come in here, Carl. Get out if you can."

Blankton turned around, his cold eyes challenging the serried faces which made a kind of wall before him.

"I'll take six of you with me," he said, and he was not boasting. Now that his moment of destiny had caught up with him, Carl Blankton lost the sadistic fear which had driven him for most of his adult life.

He knew that he was going to die, and strangely the very knowledge wiped away his fear. He was perfectly calm, detached. He stood there selecting the six men. Contrary to general practice he carried six loads in his Colt's. After he completed the selection he said mockingly:

"Start the ball, boys. We can't all live forever."

They watched him. This was a trap, a planned thing, yet they feared to spring it. A minute ago they had had the courage of numbers, but now, under the flat threat of Blankton's eyes, each man stood alone, certain that one of the bullets in Blankton's gun was meant for him.

One after another they turned away, some clustering at the card tables, some lining up against the bar. The last three were left facing him—and then, as if they realized their foolishness at the same time, they suddenly headed for the rear door, crowding each other in their hurry.

Blankton laughed, and his jeering voice cut across the heavy silence. "Rats. If I see one of you in town after tonight, he dies."

He backed away then, still too cautious to turn as he had in the other saloons, working slowly toward the street door. He never made it.

Frenchy Talbert had come around the corner from the alley and reached the door in time to see the last of the play. He drew Phil Moore's gun, and when less than ten feet separated him from the retreating man he shot Blankton squarely in the middle of the back.

Talbert stepped across the body of the man he had just shot. He still held the warm gun in his hand, and he felt quite cheerful.

"The street is open, boys. The Western Belle will be doing business within the hour."

He walked out into Railroad Avenue. A dozen men followed him. By the time he reached the corner and paused to unlock the big saloon, the group had swelled to nearly a hundred.

Watching from the safety of the railroad station waiting-room, Hartford Hull smiled to himself. They were back in control. Blankton was dead, and Joe Condon would not return to town alive. There was no one to stop them now. Dexter Springs would fall into their lap like an overripe apple.

Chapter Eighteen

The Box A herd spread out for miles. To Lucy Warner, who had only seen cattle bunched in the pens or being driven up the town streets, the sight was breath-taking.

It was still early in the season and not many herds had preceded the Box A. Some grass still remained along the trail, but the riders let their charges move slowly, feeding as they went, in a column that stretched three miles across its front.

The second section of the herd was less than half a day behind now, so that joint crews had mingled and the animals would be driven into the shipping pens in a continuous stream.

Joe Condon was surprised to find them so close to town. The buckboard had covered less than ten miles before they picked up the point riders and learned that Pat Alder was at the headquarters camp two miles away.

Both men on point were cool, reserved in their greeting although Joe had known them both for a long time. The breach between himself and the Box A was very wide.

It seemed even wider when he pulled up to the chuck wagon. Pat Alder looked at him as if they had never met and then stomped away.

Kern Alder was present, however, and he

guessed that she had ridden out from town that morning. The copy of the *Sentinel* which he saw on the ground helped to explain her visit. She had brought the newspaper along to show to Pat.

Kern came forward as he stepped down and offered Lucy his hand, and Kern's voice was sharp as she called after her father.

"Lucy Warner is here. Come over here and make her welcome."

Pat Alder could be brusque with men, but it was not in him to be rude to a woman. He came back. He ignored Condon but he said to Lucy, "*You* are welcome, Ma'am. I'm glad you came out. You can tell your father that we'll reach the pens with the first cattle sometime tomorrow and that three days should see them all delivered."

Lucy was busy looking around her. "I've never seen so many animals in my life!"

Pat's mouth twisted. "I'll be glad to see the last of them. You can get real tired of a steer in three thousand miles."

Kern laughed. "And six months from now you'll be r'aring to bring up another herd."

"Not here." His big jaw jutted at Joe Condon. "We're coming in armed," he said, "and you'd better have that murdering deputy out of town if you don't want him hung."

The cook and helper had stopped to listen, and from the tail of his eye Condon saw them edge closer. If he were alone this could develop into trouble, but he knew Alder would not allow anything to start while the girls were here. It helped him to speak boldly.

He said, "You've known me a long time, Pat. You know I don't like killing, and I don't like trouble, and there isn't going to be any trouble at the Springs as long as I'm wearing this star."

They glared at each other. It was not the first time he and Pat had differed, but never before had the issue been deadly serious.

"Your crew will be treated like any other crew," Joe said. "They will take off their guns the minute they ride into town, and they will leave them off until they ride out. That's final."

"And if we don't?"

"I'll personally jail every one I catch. This game is for keeps, Pat. You'll have to kill me to stop me."

Lucy Warner had never seen Condon like this. She glanced at Kern Alder, and to her astonishment she caught a small pleased smile as it flickered across the beautiful face. Why, the girl was enjoying this. She wanted them to fight for her entertainment.

Lucy took a half step forward.

"Mr. Alder," she said, "if you won't listen to Joe, listen to me. There are a lot of decent people in Dexter Springs, people who regretted the death of your man as much as you do. Don't turn our town into a shambles. Joe is trying his best to handle a bad situation. Help him, don't fight him."

Alder loomed over, red and shaggy and huge, and he came as near rudeness as he could with a woman. "I understand how you feel," he said. "You can straighten things out. Condon is your man, so make him have some sense. If he'll turn this Blankton over to us, I promise you there will be no trouble. No gun will be worn in town and not one of my riders will enter a saloon or even stay in town overnight."

Condon picked it up before Lucy could reply. He said, "You know I can't do that, Pat. You would never give up one of your own crew even if he were the worst murderer alive."

Alder grunted.

"And Blankton isn't that. He was being shot at. The real people to blame are Frenchy Talbert and the gambler Yale. I have them in jail."

"Give them to me."

"I can't do that either. I'm a law officer. If I can prove anything against them I'll send them to prison but—" He was talking to empty air. Pat Alder had snorted and walked away.

Kern said, "You're wasting your time, Joe. You might as well go back to town. In fact I'll ride back with you. My horse threw a shoe coming out and he's a little lame."

"I'm surprised that anyone from the Box A would ride with me," Condon said stiffly.

She laughed at him and turned to Lucy. "You're lucky you have your handsome editor. You don't have to put up with this bullheaded cowboy. I thought I might marry him once. In fact, if it comes to the worst I'll probably marry him in the end. But you have to understand Joe. You have to know how to handle him."

Condon knew that his face was red beneath the heavy tan. At the moment he could have strangled Kern with his two hands. He stalked angrily toward the buckboard. Behind him he heard Kern say. "Men are all alike. You have to handle them. The minute you treat one as an equal you've lost your power over them." She laughed again and skipped gaily toward the buckboard with Lucy Warner following uncertainly in her wake.

They drove in silence, moving easily through the scattered herd so not to stampede them. The steers were being pushed faster than they had been on the trail, but still not fast enough to melt the tallow off of them.

It took almost two hours before they passed the point riders and Condon judged that they were not over five miles at most from the pens.

He had little time to do anything. The showdown was plodding up the trail behind him, not fast, but moving with relentless steadiness.

They were driving through a break in the row of sand hills, where a small creek had cut a path across the rolling terrain, when two riders pulled clear of a thicket of cottonwood to their right and closed in, one on each side of the team.

Both men had drawn their neckerchiefs up across the lower part of their faces, and Joe Condon took this to be a holdup. He almost laughed, considering the very small sum of money he carried.

One rider grabbed the reins and held the nervous team. The other rode to the side of the buckboard.

"All right, Marshal. Step down." Only then did he realize that they knew who he was. Both girls had been staring dumfounded at the masked men.

Involuntarily Lucy said, "No," and started to stand up. The man on the horse beside the buckboard reached over with his free hand and pushed her back in the seat.

"Sit down and act sensible and you won't get hurt, Ma'am. We just want a little talk with the marshal."

Condon got to his feet. With the girls in the wagon he had no intention of going for his gun. But Kern Alder chose this moment to take over the lines which Condon had dropped. Neither of the masked riders was watching her, so she bent forward carefully, lifted the lines, catching them in her left hand. She edged her right hand down along the dangling ends. Suddenly she rose up, yelling at the horses, bringing the ends of the lines over to snap smartly across their rumps.

They jumped, startled, breaking the grip that one man had on the left horse's bridle, rearing so that their pawing front hoofs knocked his mount sidewise.

The scared horse went to his knees, throwing his rider over his head. The team plunged on. A hind hoof struck the fallen man's head, killing him instantly. The second man brought his horse around with a curse. Kern was still standing, screeching at the top of her voice as the buckboard jounced over the rough ground.

Behind them the second man was spurring desperately, his gun raised. He fired once, the bullet cutting over their heads. The second shot hit Kern in the back. She reeled and started to fall from the careening wagon. Condon reached out to grab an arm. He barely caught her. Off balance, he dragged and jerked her clear of the spinning wheels. Then he lifted her already limp body across him into Lucy's lap.

"Hold her," he shouted.

Ignoring the racing horses and the dangling lines, he twisted his body, drew and aimed his gun. His first shot struck the following horse in the head. The animal somersaulted in the air, pitching his rider to the ground.

Condon dropped the gun and leaned far forward to catch the lines. Then, straining backward with all his might, he tried to check the frightened horses. They traveled a good quarter of a mile before he got them under control.

He swung down fast, not trusting them, leading them to a stand of cottonwood along the creek and tying them tight before he went back to the wagon.

Kern was entirely limp in Lucy's arms. Lucy said in a shaken voice, "I think she's dead."

"Not yet," Kern Alder whispered.

Joe lowered her to the ground as gently as he could, and the amount of blood that stained her dress shocked him. The wound in her back was close under the left shoulder blade and he wondered how the heavy bullet could have missed the heart.

"We've got to get her to a doctor, quick."

Her eyes opened and there was the barest trace of the old smile he knew so well. "Kiss me, Joe."

He kissed her gently, his lips barely brushing hers, and she said against them, "No doctor. I won't last a mile. This is it, Joe."

He had trouble with words. His throat muscles were stiff. "Sure you will."

Her head moved slightly and she saw Lucy. "He's about the best there is and I treated him rough. Make up for it, will you?" She coughed. There was a sudden rush of blood from her mouth and she was dead.

Joe stared down at her, not believing it, feeling empty now, completely washed out. She had been a part of his life. She had left marks upon him.

With all her selfishness, her lack of real feeling for others, she had still offered him something which he would never quite find in anyone else.

Slowly he straightened out her arms and legs and clothing. He couldn't think clearly, couldn't decide what to do next. It was Lucy who took over with a briskness foreign to her, as if she had gained a certain decisive quality from the dead girl.

"Her father will have to know."

"Of course."

"And those men—are they dead?"

He did not know and did not care. The whole thing had been so fruitless. If Kern had not tried to drive away she would still be alive. . . . And then it hit him with full impact. Kern had saved him. She had given her life for his.

They drove back to where the pursuing gunman's horse had gone down. The man had dragged himself to one side. He sat up as Condon jumped down, gun in hand.

"My leg's broke." The voice was a pleading whine.

"Who hired you?" Condon said.

The man turned sullen. Condon retrieved his gun from the grass fifty feet away. As he straightened up he saw two horsemen in the southern distance. They were the point riders, coming over to investigate.

• • •

It was a silent, stony-faced group which rode into the Box A camp. Pat Alder had been sitting beside the chuck wagon, grieving, ever since the news reached him. He stood up. He moved forward, shambling. He stood gazing down at his daughter in a kind of dazed, unbelieving way as if his mind refused to credit what his eyes told him. Then he looked at Condon, but it was Lucy Warner who told him what had happened.

Lucy took Pat's gnarled, rope broken hands in both her own, and told of his daughter's courage, of how she had driven the team against the mounted man, of how she had saved Condon's life.

When she finished Pat Alder lifted his daughter's body in his arms and laid her on the blanket beside the fire. Then he walked to the killer who had been brought in by the point riders.

The man sat woodenly, his broken leg stretched out before him, his face gray with pain and fear. He had no hope. He knew already that in the minds of these rock-faced Texans his fate was sealed. Still, he tried.

"I didn't mean to kill your girl," he told Pat Alder. "We were going to let her go. We wanted him." He nodded toward Condon.

"Who hired you?" Alder said.

"Why should I tell you? I'm dead anyway."

"You're dead, all right. But you'll tell me before you die or there won't be an unbroken bone in your body."

Sweat made a sickly sheen across the pallor of the man's face. "What do I owe Frenchy?" he wondered aloud. "I wasn't even paid."

Condon said, "It wasn't Frenchy who hired you. He's in jail. Who did hire you? Who's behind Talbert?"

The man's puzzlement was genuine. "There ain't no one behind Talbert. He's the boss as far as I know. I went and talked to him through the jail window."

Condon turned his back. There seemed to be only one way to pierce the blanket of secrecy which surrounded Talbert's actions. He made up his mind to beat the truth out of the saloon man if he had to kill him in the process.

They buried Kern beside the small creek. Lucy said timidly that she should be taken to the little graveyard in town, but Pat Alder would not have it so.

"I wouldn't have her in that stinking town," he growled. "I wouldn't bury a dog there."

Afterward he stood beside Condon, not speaking for a long while. Finally he said, "She was a good girl," as if he wanted and needed confirmation.

"She was the best," Joe Condon said. "There was no one like her."

"This Talbert. You have him in jail. Give him to me."

"I'll handle him, Pat."

Alder did not seem to hear. "We'll be in," he said. "You'd better go on ahead. I wouldn't want Miss Lucy around when it happens."

Condon knew he was talking about the killer. He nodded. Even if he wanted to save the man's life, he could do nothing about it. Most of the Box A crew was gathered around the fire, silently watching him talk with Alder.

He went over to Lucy. "We'd better go," he said.

She understood. She nodded and climbed into the buckboard. They drove off briskly through the vast herd. The sun was well down in the west and Condon wanted to get clear of the cattle before darkness.

Neither of them spoke. A strained mutual awareness made them both uneasy. They knew that certain things had to be said, but neither was yet ready to speak out.

Once clear of the cattle, Condon whipped the horses into a trot. They bounced across the uneven ground, seeing the lights of the town glow below them as they mounted the last rise of swelling hills and dropped down toward the line of railroad two miles away. They came in the southeast end, since the trail led to the cattle pens and loading chutes, and crossed Railroad Avenue on Sixth.

Out of habit Joe Condon looked down along the wide street. Then he jerked the jaded team to an abrupt halt.

Five blocks away, the lights of the Western Belle blazed through their windows, revealing a crowd of men that reached almost to the Railroad tracks. Even at the distance Condon could hear their shouts and laughter.

"What's going on?" Lucy murmured.

"I don't know," he said grimly, "but I'll find out."

He whipped up the team, clattering across to the Denver Street entrance of the livery and into the runway. The barn man came forward as he helped Lucy down, saying, "Marshal, where have you been? There's hell to pay."

"What's happened?"

"Carl Blankton's dead. Talbert's out of jail and he's opened the Western Belle again. Everyone this side of the tracks is scared. They're talking about hiding under the beds."

Condon turned to Lucy. "I'll have Bob here drive you home." He nodded to the barn man and headed for the door. Lucy called, "Joe, be careful!" but he did not hear her.

Chapter Nineteen

The marshal's office was dark. A voice halted him as he came through the door.

"Stay where you are!"

He said, "It's Condon," and heard a long-drawn breath.

"Joe? It's *you?*"

"Of course it's me. Light a light. What the hell is going on here anyhow?"

He heard a match scratched, and saw Phil Moore outlined in the tiny flame. Then the big lamp's wick caught, dissolving the shadows from the room.

It showed him Harvey Blankton at the open window, a shotgun in his hand. Phil Moore was just replacing the chimney on the lamp.

"Have you heard? Carl's dead. Talbert shot him in the back."

Condon nodded. "How in hell did Talbert get out?"

Phil Moore touched the side of his head where a swelling bruise still showed through his thin hair. "I got too close to the door. He grabbed my gun. He got my keys."

Condon stared at him bleakly. "All right. Tell it the way it happened."

Phil Moore tried to stare him down and failed.

His eyes fell away. He was scared, shaken. In fumbling words he told exactly what had happened.

Condon cursed him wickedly. "I should kill you, but I haven't got time. Now, what's happened since?"

It was Harvey Blankton who said, "Everything. Talbert reopened the Western Belle and all the toughs gathered around him. Then he sent word here that if either Phil or I tried to cross Railroad Avenue we were dead. Along in the middle of the afternoon a rumor went through town that you'd been killed, and when you didn't show up by dark we believed it. What else could we do?" He sounded a little guilty, as if he feared that Condon would blame him along with Phil Moore.

Condon said, "There's nothing you could have done that I know of. Have you seen the mayor?"

"He and Hull were here earlier. Both of them told us to stay out of sight and not stir things up. I don't know where they are now, but people were gathering at the mayor's house."

"All right. Stay here. Put your lights out and if they try to come after you, slip out the back door. You aren't going to help things by getting yourselves killed."

He took off without waiting for an answer, heading down Second at a half run. He saw the blaze of lights long before he reached the house, and realized that it was filled with people and that there were men in the yard.

Somebody challenged him as he reached the gate, and he stopped, calling his name.

The shock of hearing Condon's voice almost stunned Hartford Hull, for it was he standing in the darkness, a shotgun in his hands. All evening it had amused him to play his double part, to sit in the council and debate ways and means of protecting the people north of the tracks from the mob prowling from one saloon to another south of Railroad Avenue.

He knew that there would be no real attack; it was not part of his plan to destroy the town. But the more he could make these people believe their danger, the more he could control their actions. In the midafternoon he had volunteered to cross the street for a conference with Talbert, ostensibly to get the saloon man to call off his wolves, actually to set their plans in the privacy of Talbert's office. Then he learned that Frenchy had put two men on the marshal's trail with orders to follow him wherever he went and ambush him.

Talbert had not known that Condon would leave town, but this development had played directly into their hands. Hull returned to the mayor with the rumor that Condon was dead.

The news had shaken Boyce. For the first time the little man lost part of his nerve. Being aware that neither Phil Moore nor Harvey Blankton could provide the strength he needed to control the situation, Boyce had called some forty merchants and their wives to his home, forming a kind of citizens' committee for their joint protection. They had appointed Hull as the leader, relying on his wartime military experience, and at that point Hull had the situation completely in hand.

But now, here was Joe Condon. . . .

Hartford Hull recovered quickly in the darkness.

"Joe!" he said warmly. "My God, man, we heard you were dead!"

"I'm not." Condon brushed past him, hurrying up the walk with Hull at his heels. "But the men who tried are, and they killed Kern Alder by accident."

The news jarred Hull again, and he took a third blow when he stepped inside and heard Condon say to the mayor, "You can stop worrying. Pat Alder is on his way up with twenty riders. As soon as they get here I'll clean out that bunch around the Western Belle and close every saloon along Railroad Avenue."

Hull said in a disbelieving voice, "You mean Alder will fight with you after the trouble you two had?"

"I do," Condon said. "Those two men Talbert sent after me killed Alder's daughter."

A clammy silence settled down upon the

crowded room. To these merchants, the daughter of a Texas cattle baron was a valued customer, a privileged personage, a woman above threat of attack. Her death touched them more than the news that Blankton and Cap Lennox and Pete Ortman had been murdered. If she had died of violence, then their wives and daughters were not safe.

No one noticed Hartford Hull as he slipped from the room. Even if his absence were noted, it would be assumed that he had returned to his post in the yard. But Hull did not linger there. He hurried along Second until he reached the corner of Railroad Avenue, then called to a member of the shouting crowd and sent him with a message to Frenchy Talbert. Condon was at the mayor's house. Condon had to die before Alder's men arrived.

Then Hull rushed back to his post in the yard.

The mob came up both Second and Third. Despite the liquor they had drunk, these south-of-the-tracks toughs managed to put on an orderly and purposeful march.

The men inside the mayor's house heard them long before they arrived, and Hull built the tension higher when he stepped in with a strained, worried expression.

"We'd better get the women and kids out of here," he said. "And we'd better do it fast."

Boyce was steady, the rest of the council

members inclined to panic. He gave his orders and the women with their children stole through the rear door and across the dark yard. Only Mrs. Boyce refused to go.

The mob advanced along the street, a dozen flaming torches lighting their noisy progress. Boyce started for the front door. His wife elbowed forward to seize his arm.

"Jerome, no. Don't go out. They'll kill you. They'll—"

He put her aside, not gently, and went along the hall. Hull stopped him near the door. "Let the marshal go, Jerome. It's his business."

Condon started toward them.

"Stay where you are," Jerome Boyce said. "I'm the mayor. I'm the one to talk to them."

He went on then, thrusting the front door open and coming out onto the porch as the leaders of the unwieldly crowd came against his light fence, splintering it by the very weight of their numbers.

He stood there, a small, strangely commanding figure, and the very fact that he was alone made them pause.

"What's the meaning of this?" His voice cut through the night, loud and demanding and steady. "Go back where you came from."

"Condon! We want Condon! Where's the marshal? Where's the butcher?"

"I haven't an idea."

"You're a liar." It was Frenchy Talbert, in the

forefront of the mob. "He's inside. Bring him out before we burn your place."

But Joe Condon was no longer in the house. He shifted across the rear yard, stopping suddenly as he saw someone move in the darkness. "Who is it?" he whispered.

"Joe! Joe, it's Lucy."

"Good Lord, girl, what are you doing here?"

"Some of the women ran to our house. I came over to see what was happening."

"Boyce is talking to them from the porch, Lucy. Listen."

Through the night they heard Talbert shout. "You're through, Boyce. You and Joe Condon made all this trouble. You're leaving town, first thing in the morning."

The little mayor's tone was deceptively mild. "I am?"

"We'll elect a new mayor. You and Joe Condon started all the trouble here."

"And whom will you elect?"

There was a pause. Then Talbert said, "I'm in business here, like you are. I don't want trouble, but I was arrested and closed without cause. I want someone who'll be fair to both sides. What about Hartford Hull? You surely can't object to him, and the boys south of the tracks know he's fair and honest."

Lucy drew a breath of relief. "If they let Hartford take over everything will be all right.

He's a good manager. He'll stop this trouble."

"Nothing will stop it until Pat Alder gets here," Condon said, and then before she realized it he was gone, fading back into the darkness. She would have followed, but she did not know which direction he had taken. Reluctantly she stayed there, hidden, listening.

On the surface a compromise was reached. Boyce resigned and appointed Hull as acting mayor as his last official act. Hull made a short speech to the crowd. He said that Joe Condon was suspended pending an investigation, and appointed two men as acting marshals. Then he walked to a corner of the porch and talked to Frenchy Talbert in a low voice.

"Condon's gone. I don't know where he is, but I've told Bunch and Forster to arrest him on sight."

He nodded at the two men he had just appointed marshals. The choice had been excellent. Bunch and Forster had led the successful attack on the beef herd. But still, Talbert was worried.

"How many men has this Alder got?" he asked.

"Condon said about twenty. If they ride in, Bunch will try to make them give up their guns. They won't, so he'll deputize every man in sight and try to arrest them. The only thing we don't want is for Alder to get killed before he collects that gold for his cattle. We want that gold and the cows too."

Talbert smiled, then. "It's in the bank," he said.

They looked at each other for a long moment of understanding. The risks were great, but the rewards were high. Hull went back into the house, well pleased with himself. The mob was making its noisy way down the street.

Lucy said, "I was never prouder of you."

He waved his hand as if he had done nothing at all. "The trouble is over. If Condon had used his head it might never have started. You can't arrest a man like Talbert. He has too many friends."

She started to protest, but he had already turned away. Outside, Frenchy Talbert was giving orders, posting guards at the edge of town to warn him of Alder's approach, and perhaps to catch Condon. But he was too late. Joe Condon had already ridden out.

Chapter Twenty

It was nearly three o'clock in the morning. The guard was watching the trail which came up from the south to wind around the stock pens and enter Sixth Street. He heard horses, but the number puzzled him. He had been told to expect twenty riders, and unless his ears had gone bad there were only two out there now.

He mounted, but he made the mistake of lingering until the pair loomed suddenly out of the darkness.

"Stay where you are!" Joe Condon's voice cut at him.

The guard tried to wheel and cut out, but Condon closed with him before he got the horse clear around. Condon grabbed the collar of his coat and yanked him free of the saddle and he hit the ground hard.

The others rode in by twos, slowly, quietly, until they formed a tight ring about him.

"What are you doing here?" Condon said harshly.

The man wiped his mouth with the back of a dirty hand. He was scared, not knowing what would happen. He blurted, "You ain't marshal any more. Boyce resigned and Hull is acting mayor. Bunch and Forster are the marshals and I'm a deputy."

Pat Alder grunted. "We don't need any badge to do what we're going to do. We should hang you here, but we haven't got the time. Hit the grit along the tracks. If I see you again I'll kill you." He reached down and pulled the gun from the guard's holster and flipped it to one of his men.

They walked their horses into town. The celebration had been dying gradually. Men worn out by excitement and liquor had sought their beds, but there was still a full crowd in the Western Belle when the front door opened and two riders came in.

The first bartender looked up. He noted their heavy tans, their dusty clothes, and he stiffened a little. He moved forward, saying, "I'll keep your guns, boys," while at the same time he signalled to Bunch who stood beside one of the rear card tables.

The taller newcomer stood a good six feet. He had gray eyes and a long, narrow face. His hair had not been cut in a month and grew down under the edge of his hat, giving him a slightly Indian look.

"We aren't staying," he said. "Just a drink and we'll be on our way."

The door behind him opened and three more riders came in. The bartender froze. Bunch left the card table and moved toward the front of the room. Behind him, Joe Condon stepped through the rear door. Joe Condon was well inside the room before anyone saw him.

The bartender stood pat, a bottle half raised in his hand. He held that pose, not daring to break it, because the newcomers had drawn their guns and fanned out, dominating the room. The tall man nodded to Condon.

"All right, Joe, do your stuff."

Condon was already striding toward the office door. He threw it open with his free hand, his other holding his gun ready. The room beyond was empty.

"Where's Talbert?" he barked at the bartender.

The man dropped his bottle and flinched at the noise.

"I don't know."

"Better find out quick," the tall rider said, and shot the bottle into splinters that sprayed the bartender's legs.

Condon cursed him. The shot might well warn Talbert, and he had hoped to gather in the saloon man without killing. But he could not really blame the rider. The Box A had ridden in spoiling for trouble, with a deep-down grievance against this town.

Pat Alder burst through the outer door like a bull charging into a pen. "Who shot? Where's this Talbert?"

Condon told him what had happened.

Alder turned on the bartender, who was

standing on one foot, gingerly rubbing the calf of one leg against the gashed skin of the other because he did not dare bend down and use his hands.

"All right, where's Talbert? And stand on both your goddam feet!"

The apron stood on both his goddam feet. "He went up to the marshal's office with Forster. I guess they're still there."

Condon spoke to the Texans. "Stay here. Don't let anyone leave." He followed Alder out into the street. All up and down its dark length Box A riders were guarding the entrances of the saloons, keeping the patrons penned inside.

Condon said, "You stay here too, Pat. If any trouble starts it will be on this street."

"It was my girl who got killed," Pat Alder grumbled.

"I loved her too," Condon said, and meant it. He knew now that a man can love two women in different ways. "Talbert belongs to me."

The older man studied Condon's face, gauntly outlined in the light from the Western Belle doorway. "He's yours," he said, and clumped heavily away.

Condon crossed the wide street and started up First toward the city hall. Sound behind him made him whirl, dropping his hand to his gun. Two of the Texans were following him.

"Where do you think you're going?" he said.

"Pat's orders, Joe. Just in case."

He knew he couldn't send them back. If he tried it they would refuse. Without another word he led the way northward. He saw lights in both the mayor's and the marshal's offices and he hesitated. Then he told one rider to watch the front door and sent the second around to the rear with orders to stop anyone who tried to leave through the alley. After that he moved to the doorway of his own office and peered inside.

Forster sat in a chair tilted back against the wall behind the desk. His head had fallen forward so that his chin rested on his breastbone. He was asleep, and he was alone in the office.

For a minute Condon stood there, debating what to do. He could wake Forster, disarm him and lock him in one of the cells, but if Forster acted up the noise might warn whoever was in the mayor's office. He suspected it was Talbert, and Talbert interested him a lot more than Forster did. Still, Forster had a gun and he did not want an armed man at his back.

He stepped quietly into the room and had Forster's gun before the man was thoroughly awake. Forster raised his head and stared up at him blearily.

"Condon!" Forster snapped fully awake and his head came back with a jerk to thump against the wall. He started to get up and Joe Condon shoved him back.

"Sit quiet."

The man's weak mouth worked to form words and finally he got them out. "You're suspended. I'm marshal now."

"And I'm holding your gun."

Forster tried to sneer. "And Talbert has a hundred men."

"I brought a few back with me," Condon said quietly. "Step out on the street and you'll get your head blown off. The game is over. Where's Talbert?"

The man licked his lips. "He was in the mayor's office."

"What's he doing in there?"

"I don't know."

"Alone?"

"I think so."

"All right, get on your feet and move back to the cells. No tricks." He choused Forster into the jail corridor and along it toward the rear cell. At the cell door Forster started to enter, then made his belated bid for freedom. He whirled, wrenched open the rear door of the building and flung himself through.

Condon's yell of warning reached the Texan in the alley before Forster did. He saw the door sweep open, saw Forster plunging toward him. And he fired.

The heavy slug caught Forster squarely in the face, but the momentum of his headlong rush hurtled him on so that his lifeless body struck the rider, carrying him to the ground. He was still trying to roll free when Joe Condon pulled Forster off of him.

Forster was dead. Condon ran back into the building.

Frenchy Talbert heard the shot. It crashed almost under the window of the marshal's office. It lifted him out of his chair and brought him across the room in time to see Condon dash into the building, though not in time to shoot Condon. So Frenchy did the next best thing.

He drew his gun and shot the Texan who was bending over Forster's body. Then he calmly shot out the light on the corner of the desk, heedless that the spilled oil might fire the building. And after that he smashed the glass of the window with the barrel of his revolver and dropped through to the alley.

The big temptation was to race to the Western Belle and get his men, but common sense told him that Condon was in the city hall and Condon was his main source of danger.

He would never have a better chance to corner him.

Condon was halfway through the city clerk's office, between the jail and the mayor's office, when he heard the two shots and the splintering of glass.

He checked himself, then rushed on to throw

open the connecting door. The room reeked with the smell of hot oil and cordite fumes, but he did not see Talbert.

He stood peering around into the darkness. Talbert could still be in the room, waiting for him to appear, but he heard no sound to indicate this.

He took one cautious step, then another. Nothing happened. He moved quickly to the shattered window and peered into the darkness below.

The path of light from the still open jail door showed him two huddled, motionless bodies, one lying across the other. But he did not make the mistake of dropping into the alley. He ran back through the building and out the front door.

The rider he had left on Second called to him as he emerged and he answered, "Watch it. Talbert's somewhere in the alley. He got Jim Trent." He saw the man approach and warned, "Keep back. Watch the alley mouth. If he comes out, get him. I'm going to circle the block."

He turned, running around the corner and down Denver to where the bisecting alley opened at the far side of the city hall.

Its length was blackness, and somewhere in that blackness Talbert must be waiting. If he had gone the other way he would have come out on Railroad Avenue, and Pat Alder's men were guarding the wide street with hawk-like vigilance, ready to close in on anything that moved.

He sent his voice along it, hearing it echo back to him, hollowly. “Come on out, Talbert. The play is over. I’ve got your men on Railroad blocked. You can’t get away.”

A blob of flame blossomed in the alley depths. The heavy slug struck the corner of the building at his right. He ducked instinctively, screening himself by the building, and heard Talbert’s mocking laugh.

“Come and get me, Marshal. I can see you against the sky the minute you step in.”

Condon did not answer. The logical thing would be to retreat, to get more help and dig the man out building by building, shadow by shadow.

But if he left, Talbert might slip through into the upper residential section while he was gone.

The structure to the left of the alley was single storied, with a false front that gave it the appearance of double its actual height. A wooden awning set on posts ran out over the sidewalk, almost above the hitch-rail. He backed to the rail and stepped up on it. Getting his hands over the edge of the wooden awning, he lifted himself to its shed-like slant. He walked upward until he reached the false front, jumped, and caught his fingers over the upper edge.

For a long moment he clung there, his fingertips supporting his full weight. Then he dropped back for a second try. This time he secured a better grip, and he raised himself until he could throw his right foot over the top.

The front was made of boards mounted on a two-by-four frame. It swayed dangerously as Condon climbed, but he managed to get up and over, dropping to the safety of the roof.

He moved along the edge on the alley side, careful that not enough of his head showed beyond the edge to silhouette him against the starlit sky. But suddenly he stopped, listening. At first the sound was hard to identify, and then he realized that Frenchy Talbert had acted upon the same idea that had occurred to him. Talbert had caught the roof edge and was dragging himself upward.

His head appeared. Then he threw one leg over the roof lip and hauled himself over until he could roll his body onto the flat surface. He came to his knees, not ten feet from Condon.

Condon said, "Hold it, Frenchy."

Talbert jerked himself sidewise, drawing his gun, rolling as if he were trying to pitch himself back into the depths of the alley. He came to his knees at the brink of the roof and snapped a shot. It went over Condon's head.

Condon fired in return, and knew even as he squeezed the trigger that he had missed. He saw Talbert disappear over the roof edge. He ran forward, trying to see into the darkness below.

Somewhere a voice was calling his name, and

he guessed that it was the rider he had left on the street. And then he saw movement below him.

He jumped, landing squarely on Talbert. He heard Talbert moan and he muttered hoarsely, "You've had it. Give up." He felt the body under him slacken, then felt it gather itself and twist. He did not realize Talbert had a knife until the burning stab pierced his arm.

The blade struck his muscle, driving clear through it, the point breaking the cloth of his shirt, scratching his side.

The deepness probably saved Condon's life. As he lunged away, the motion of his body tore the knife handle from Talbert's grasp. They went over together, crashing into a trash box which fell on top of them. Then Joe got his right hand around the handle of the knife which was still embedded in the muscle of his arm. He pulled it free and stabbed twice, hardly knowing what he did, and the body under him relaxed. After that he heard shouting and tall Texas shapes materialized in the gloom. They lifted him to his feet. In the flare of a sputtering match they looked down at Talbert. The saloon man was dead.

Chapter Twenty-One

A lesser man than Hartford Hull would have quit. The world he had built was falling about his ears. Talbert was dead, and the gamblers and saloon men who had been Talbert's strength were gone—over a hundred of them, loaded on the train by Joe Condon and Pat Alder's men. But the thought of quitting never entered Hull's head.

Instead, he schemed on as he stood watching the Box A herds being driven onto a bed ground north of town. There were too many of them for the loading pens, and the trampled ground along the railroad provided no feed whatever.

Until sufficient cars arrived, Lloyd Warner planned to hold the herds on grass. The sight of the bawling animals made Hull's eyes glisten. His investment along Railroad Avenue, which had been in Talbert's name, was lost. He no longer had any hope of seizing the gold which Pat Alder and his men were taking south to the Nations, because he dared not attack Alder's crew with his weakened strength. But the cattle—that was different. Warner had managed to hire only four men to guard the bed ground.

These four could not stop him. He would

stampede the animals north, and no one in town would follow. No one, unless Condon, Phil Moore and Harvey Blankton did.

The two deputies had come back. They had ridden out of town when Talbert took over the city hall and had not returned until the town was safe under the Box A guns. They had walked into the marshal's office, expecting to be fired, and were amazed when Condon greeted them as if nothing had happened.

"The town is clean," he told them. "There isn't a saloon open in Dexter Springs. Whether they ever reopen is up to the council. Alder is delivering his cattle and riding south. After he goes I'm leaving too."

They stared at him, not understanding. Joe did not quite understand himself. His left arm was in a sling but the healing wound did not trouble him. He just had a feeling of unrest, an edgy letdown after the worry of the past weeks. Dexter Springs would never be the same. The town's future would be more ordered, more quiet, but the gaudy, lively past seemed to keep on demanding the same tempo, the same nervous energy, for which the present offered no outlet.

He had no knowledge of Hull's plans, no way of knowing that the coming night would be wilder than any in the Springs' short history. He got his horse and rode out toward the bed ground with Blankton at his side.

“You’re a hero,” Harvey Blankton said. “The people on the street are still talking about your fight with Talbert.”

“These same people gave me no help last night,” Condon said. “If I hadn’t had Alder’s crew, Talbert would own Dexter Springs today.”

They headed toward the swirl of dust which marked the milling herd. They pulled up beside the buckboard in which Lloyd Warner sat with his crutches stacked beside him. Lucy shared the seat with her father and Hartford Hull was standing beside the wagon.

Hull masked his bitterness with a quick smile and extended his hand. “I was wrong, Joe, and I’m the first to admit it. I couldn’t believe Talbert was fool enough to try what he did.”

Condon pretended not to see the hand, and Lucy frowned unhappily. Ever since her ride with Condon she had been extremely uneasy, charging herself with disloyalty, feeling that she should tell Hull. The chance to confess had not come, however, and now here was Hull showing a certain bigness in apology, while Condon lost stature by refusing it.

Pat Alder rode up, lifting his hat to wipe the sweat and dust from his forehead.

“That’s it. I hope your cars get here this week. If they don’t you’ll have to move farther out for more grass.”

“I wired again this morning,” Warner said. “If

you'll ride down to the bank we'll square up. The tally's finished."

Alder nodded and rode around to Joe's side. "I can use you," he said in a low voice. Once it would have been an order. Now it was more of a plea. "I've got those two leases in the Nations. I was going to put Rick on one and run the other myself. Now I find I want to go back to Texas. I want to be around things I know, and people I know. I haven't got much left to live for."

Joe Condon found it hard to turn this man down. He glanced around as if for help, and his eyes met those of Lucy Warner. He asked a question silently and got no answer. She let her gaze fall to the reins in her gloved hands, knowing that color had surged up into her cheeks and betrayed her emotion.

Hull observed this and wondered about it, for he was a man who habitually noted small things and stored them away for future consideration. He allowed himself one more look at the cattle which he already considered were his, and then without another word he walked away.

Condon watched him with a sharpened curiosity.

Alder said, "Hang up that fool badge and come back and do a man's work for a change."

Condon shifted in the saddle. "I'm sorry, Pat. I kind of thought I'd branch out for myself."

"A hardscrabble outfit," Alder said impatiently.

"Eating sagebrush and dust, nursing a hundred head. That's no way to start."

"A man has to start sometime."

"Come with me. When I die there's no one left. You and Rick can split the outfit."

It was a tempting offer. It meant that one day he would be half owner of a huge spread of ranches running from the thorny brush country clear up through the Nations. He sensed that Lucy was anxiously awaiting his reply. He knew instinctively that if he rode down the trail they would probably never see each other again.

"I can't see it, Pat."

Alder had played a lot of poker. Alder knew when he held a busted hand. "Your business," he said tonelessly, and pulled his horse around.

Warner shifted in his seat. "I got to get down to the bank to pay Alder off."

"I'll walk back," his daughter said. "It's only a mile."

He frowned at her, not understanding, but he made no protest when she climbed from the buckboard.

After Warner had driven away Joe Condon handed his reins to Harvey Blankton and stepped from the saddle. "Take him back, Harv. I'll walk in with Lucy."

Blankton registered mild surprise, then swung away. They stood for a while, just watching the massive herd. Most of the animals had settled down and were already chewing their cuds. They were spread out for nearly as far as the eye could see, the riders Warner had hired circling slowly, quieting their charges. Hull seemed to have vanished. They were alone.

Lucy said, "I wanted to talk to you. I hoped you would understand."

He nodded without speaking.

"Why did you turn down Pat Alder's offer?"

"Don't you know?"

She blushed, but she said, "No, Joe, I don't know."

"You did know, out there on the trail."

She did not deny it. "I've tried to explain to Hartford ever since, but somehow I can't find words."

"I'll tell him."

"No," she said quickly. "It's something that I have to do." She reached out timidly and touched his hand as they reached the edge of town. "I'm going home. Don't come with me. I want a chance to think, alone."

She turned up the side street then, and he watched her until she reached the second corner and passed out of his sight. Afterward he moved on toward the city hall. He knew that he should be well content. His job was done. The town was under full control, and he had no real doubt as to what Lucy's final choice would be.

And yet he seethed with restlessness. He had

this spooky feeling that trouble still stirred below the placid surface. It was the instinct which Cap Lennox had bred into him, the true lawman's reflex which you learned not to ignore if you wanted to go on living.

He tried to associate the feeling with one person, or one event, and failed. I'm turning into an old woman, he thought. I'm starting at shadows which are not there. It's high time I quit.

As he passed the bank he saw the buckboard and Alder's horse at the rail before the building. He stopped as Alder came out, followed by Warner, still on crutches. A wagon came up the street and he watched Alder and two of his men transfer the gold to its worn box.

Warner said, "First time I ever paid off a man without a drink to seal the bargain. There's a bottle at the house if you'll be kind enough to join me."

The cattleman shook his head. "I'm leading out a dry crew. The boys have played along and I'll have no drink without them." He lifted his heavy body into the saddle and turned to look at Condon. Then without a word or sign, he pulled the horse around and rode away.

A deep, haunting sense of loss came over Joe Condon. His oldest tie had just broken. He had parted with his past.

He helped Lloyd Warner into the buckboard, then lingered listlessly on the sidewalk while the cattle buyer drove away. He walked alone to the marshal's office and found both Moore and Harvey Blankton waiting for him. He crossed the office, took off his badge and laid it on the desk.

"I'm resigning," he said. "I spoke to Boyce this morning. Phil is to be acting marshal until the council meets."

The startled Moore began his stammered thanks. Condon cut him short.

"Just remember your mistakes, Phil. And don't make the same ones again."

He left the office, shouldering the weight of loneliness. The hush of early evening was on the streets. He paused briefly on the corner observing in all directions as he had so often done in the past, but there was a difference now. He no longer wore the star and what men did along these streets was not his affair. Phil Moore and young Blankton would patrol the quieted town.

He walked toward the hotel, ate a solitary meal, and then climbed to his room. But the curse of restlessness was still upon him. He went back downstairs and out into the night, ending finally at the livery where he got his horse.

He rode out then, hardly conscious of which direction he took, but with the certainty growing upon him that something was about to happen.

Chapter Twenty-Two

Hull's men moved with quiet and planned precision. Hull had watched the Box A crew leave, with the wagon bearing the gold in their midst and had sent a rider to follow to make sure that they were actually headed south.

These men had not belonged to Talbert's collection of barroom toughs. They were riders from the ranch he had established to the north. Therefore they had not been caught in Condon's dragnet. They had stayed in camp, twenty miles north, awaiting Hull's signal to swoop down on the herds.

They were a choice crew of roughnecks recruited from the outlaws who infested the Nations and the Missouri border. Most of them were wanted in a dozen states and the chance of settling on Hull's ranch and having the protection of an organized crew had great appeal for them.

They rode silently toward the bed grounds. The plan was to capture Warner's night riders, preferably without a shot, and head the animals northward with as little noise as possible.

Once the herd was in motion, Hull had little fear that they would be stopped. He knew the character of the citizens of Dexter Springs thoroughly. Not half a dozen men would join a posse to recover Warner's cattle, and by the time the cattle buyer could recruit help from the towns further east, the herds would be split into a dozen groups, each heading in a different direction until they were north of Kansas, then swinging back by a circular route to the ranch.

They struck. Two of Warner's men were dragged from the saddle before they realized that there was an enemy within miles. The third, riding too close behind his partner, saw the ring of mounted men in the light from the half moon, and fired blindly into them, dropping a horse.

Condon had been a quarter of a mile to the west of the herd, not wanting to get too close to the bedded animals for fear of spooking them.

He heard the single shot and by the time the answering volley split the night he was already riding toward the dark cluster of uneasy cattle.

Hull was cursing his men, yelling at them to get the herd started, knowing that the sound of shots would carry as far as the town.

Condon realized that someone was trying to steal Warner's cattle, although he did not know who. He saw the strays swing to the north as Hull's crew tried frantically to get the whole herd into motion.

His first thought was to break up the herd, to disperse it so widely that it would take a hundred men to gather it. He pulled around the north flank, yelling as he came, firing into the air, making the noise of a dozen men.

The cattle stopped, lowering their heads, shaking them from side to side in an effort to escape their growing, nameless fear. To the east, Hull's men were making more racket than Condon. The animals began to mill, and suddenly they broke. To Condon's horror, instead of spreading they started in a mass, back along the trail which led down toward the loading pens and town.

He did not hesitate. He sent his frightened horse directly through the press, trying to reach the leaders, trying to slow the running animals and turn them before they reached the outskirts of town.

He might have succeeded, but Hull's men were also trying to turn them, to get them headed back north. Pressing on the eastern flank, the riders succeeding only in swinging the cattle in a long curve which brought them up against the wall of the loading pens along the railroad. There they swung right and split, part of the herd charging up wide Railroad Avenue, the rest sweeping down Denver Street.

Condon's horse was caught in the pack of leaders as they made the swing. He rode for his life as the surge became a wild flight through the center of the town, an awful flood which carried everything before it, smashing building fronts, tearing down hitch-rails and awning posts and sidewalks, as destructive and uncontrollable as a cyclone.

Condon had given up trying to halt them. Right now he just wanted to get out of the way. His horse was outdistancing the cattle when suddenly, blocks ahead of him, Condon saw a white dress shine in the moonlight.

Lloyd Warner heard the first distant shot, and then the bawling of the frightened cattle. He seized his crutches and lurched toward the front door. He got there just as Lucy appeared and called to him to wait.

But Lloyd Warner did not wait. Every cent he had in the world and every bit of credit he could command was tied up in those cattle. He did not know what was happening. His one thought was to get to the livery stable, to get on a horse somehow, and find out.

He moved down the walk as fast as his wounded leg would let him, using his crutches more as a support than a means of locomotion. But he was slow and he had not quite reached the corner of Denver when his daughter caught up with him. Lucy tried to stop him, but he wrenched free and started across the street with her at his elbow.

And then they heard it—the thunder of the pounding hoofs, the splintering of wood. Lucy looked up the long street and saw the black wave running toward them. She could not see the tossing horns or the flaring nostrils in the light of the half moon, but she did not need to. The roar of doom was enough in itself.

Lloyd Warner lurched and hobbled frantically, and in his haste he fell before he had covered two thirds of the street's width. Lucy moaned in panic, but she stooped and caught him by the shoulders and tried to lift him bodily.

And in that instant Condon was at her side, out of the saddle before the running horse had more than broken its stride. He pushed her toward the row of store buildings, shouting, "Run!" He bent, caught up Lloyd Warner and stumbled after her. Coming up onto the sidewalk, he found her vainly rattling a store door. He brushed her aside, Warner still in his arms, and hit the door with the point of his shoulder. It gave. He heaved again. The lock tore away, and then they were in the sheltering darkness, rich with the smells of coffee and spice.

He pushed Lucy toward the rear as the first of the stampeding animals struck. The front window went with a crash. The building shook. One wild steer turned aside and came charging down the aisle between the counters, passed them as they huddled against the shelves of the wall. The steer took the thin boards of the rear partition with him as he broke into freedom in the alley beyond.

Then the rush of animals was gone, as quickly

as the whirlwind it resembled. Condon set Warner on his feet and they moved shakily toward the door, too stunned to speak.

Joe Condon came out onto the litter of the street first. He had a vague idea that he ought to determine definitely that the danger was past, and he certainly did not expect to see Hull. Hartford Hull was riding down the street with two of his men, cursing as he came.

He saw Condon appear in the moonlight. He jerked his horse to an air-pawing halt, and in that instant the wall of restraint behind which he had lived most of his life broke into rubble.

"God damn you, Condon!"

And then, at last, Joe Condon knew everything about Hartford Hull that he needed to know.

He stepped down into the dust of the street, every sense alert. He wanted to get away from the store front, to make certain that no stray bullet would reach Lucy.

"So it was you all the time," he said.

Hull was twenty feet away, the two riders behind him. He glared venomously down at Condon, anger making speech impossible. Except for Condon, this moment would be one of triumph, one for which he had planned so carefully over such a long time. Now the cattle were scattered. It would take days to round them up, to bunch them again into a herd. Warner could have a hundred deputies on hand to block any further move he might try to make. The game was lost and could not be recovered. Hartford Hull cleared his clogged throat with a tearing sound, and then he spoke.

"I'm going to kill you," he said. "I should have killed you a long time back."

"The way you had Cap killed?"

Hull did not even bother to answer. He pulled his horse half around as he drew his gun.

Condon's first shot hit the horse. It reared with a high, wild scream, tipping Hull out of the saddle. One of the riders snapped a shot at Condon and missed. The other rider simply spun his horse and fled down the street.

Hull had landed on his back. He rolled over, somehow coming up under the shattered hitch-rail. Then he ducked for a corner of a building where a narrow passage led back to the alley.

Condon's attention was still on the armed rider. The man fired again. This time he put his bullet through the brim of Condon's hat, taking a neat triangle from the worn felt. But then, just as Condon fired in return, he swung his horse and galloped away. Condon's bullet snipped the fold of his coat beneath his arm, but that was all.

A shot from the store corner kicked dust against Condon's boots. He retaliated with a bullet which sent splintered wood into Hull's face, driving the man deeper into the narrow passage.

Condon went after him. Early light was

breaking across the eastern sky. The dawn's dim glow made both men look huge and misshapen as they faced each other, walled in on either side by the blank board sides of the abutting stores.

As if by common consent they stood there, staring at each other, some fifteen feet separating them, each holding his gun half raised, but not firing, not even moving.

Hull's voice was hoarse with strain. "Lucky," he said. "You're so damn lucky. You're too lucky, Joe. Too lucky to live. You hear me, Joe?"

Condon did not answer. This was familiar now. This was a straightforward gunfight shaping up, and he felt scared as usual, and as usual it was good, being just scared enough to do what he had to do when the man on the prod got through flapping his mouth and made his move.

He saw the convulsive jerk of the draw. Hull brought up his gun, and he tilted his own. He knew that he had two bullets left, and he did not hurry. Even at this short distance a revolver was far from accurate.

He heard Hull's shot and felt the shock as the bullet struck his body. Its force knocked him sidewise. Hull fired a second time, wildly, coming two steps forward as he did so, a kind of wolfish satisfaction on his face, as if he had already won.

Condon steadied himself against the store wall. He shot carefully. He saw the cloth on Hull's chest jump and puff out and fall flat, and he knew he had no need to shoot again.

He turned, wondering how badly he had been hit, and stumbled out of the passage. He tripped and fell on the store porch. There was a slow burning in his right side, and he lacked strength to rise.

But then Lucy was beside him, holding him close, and everything was all right. She held him thus, fiercely, protectively, until the doctor came. Not once did she glance into the passage where Hartford Hull lay. She had forgotten the man she had once thought she would marry. Her whole attention was on Joe Condon, now and for keeps.

"It's bad," the doctor said. "I don't know if he'll make it."

But Joe Condon just smiled. He knew he could not afford to die. He had too much to live for.

Center Point Large Print
600 Brooks Road / PO Box 1
Thorndike, ME 04986-0001 USA

(207) 568-3717

US & Canada:
1 800 929-9108
www.centerpointlargeprint.com